Dark Age Woman

THE SEQUEL TO DARK AGE MAIDEN

Tom Molnar

Apple Valley Press

Printed in the United States of America

ISBN 978-0692640470

Dark Age Woman

Carina was not happy. She sat up in bed, and turned toward her husband. By the dim light of a crescent moon, she could see the outline of the man she slept with in the dark of night. He was no longer awake, she could tell by his regular breathing. A tear trickled down her cheek. She loved him dearly and yet she could not give him what he wanted—a child.

She put a hand through her thick auburn hair—hair he often commented on, especially when it gleamed a warm, reddish hue in the sun. She placed a hand at her slender waist, a waist that would not thicken with child. Father Carlo's blessing of her womb had done nothing. She thought about the morrow when they would travel to Nice. There they would take pleasure in bathing in the Mediterranean. Afterwards, she would find Oriana, the

3

healer with almost magical powers. Surely, she could make a potion to end her infertility.

Unlike some of her people, Carina did not worry excessively about the Saracens. Though Charles Martel had decisively defeated them at the Battle of Tours, they still held territory in Francia and had not been driven from their stronghold in Narbonne. Carina was confident Christians would not be overcome by Muslims, who fought a religious war of pillage and forced conversion to Allah. God was on her side, she thought. A spirited young woman wedded to a valiant knight. Surely, their prayers would be answered.

Early in the morning of the next day, they set out—forty-eight people from her manor, including her older brother, Renzo, who was now lord since their father's death. Ahead of her rode several knights, including Uberto, the man she had married eighteen months ago. He sat tall and at ease in the saddle, his dark, wavy hair and wide shoulders making her know him at first glance anywhere. And yet, he was slender through his stomach and hips. Carina could hardly find any fat on him at all, he was all firm muscle. She smiled as she thought of him in that way.

Besides the knights and their ladies, a good number of peasants traveled with them. Not the least was her spinner—smiling Gina, barely twenty-two and the mother of a toddler and seven year old Kara. All were on holiday to forget the cold of winter and to lie in the sun on the beach and maybe even swim. Thanks to Leonardo, who had become count after his Father's death, they were

4

welcome to stay in Nice before making the long return trip back to the manor. On this very night, Carina had made up her mind she would talk to Oriana.

In the middle of the afternoon, they arrived at Nice. Not stopping at the city, they continued on the short distance to the beach. Carina knew what to expect, but some of her people did not know that it was pebbles, not sand they would find on the beach. After some complaining, they unrolled their pelts and laid them down on the stones—and found them not uncomfortable as they were flat and rounded. Then they took out their picnic lunches.

Toward evening, after a fine afternoon at the beach, they were back at Leonardo's stronghold where she and Uberto were given their own chamber. Carina stood by the bed, sorting through the things they had taken with them. She was alone, for Uberto was in the great hall, most likely talking and eating with friends.

Now that she had settled into their room, Carina's foremost thought was to find Oriana. She was already excited at the prospect, for she felt sure she could help her. She opened the door and walked to her right. At the end of the hallway, she turned right and found Oriana's room. She hesitated before knocking. Sweet smelling vapors curled from the side of the closed door.

"Come in," said Oriana, "it isn't locked."

Carina opened the door and stared through the mist. Oriana was not alone. In the chamber was a girl tending a large cauldron at the fireplace. Even though the shutters were open, Carina found the smell to be sickeningly sweet.

"Carina, I am glad to see you," said Oriana, rising from where she had been kneeling near the fire. The two women embraced. By the dim light of the small window, Carina noted how gaunt and angular the healer looked. Her elongated, thin nose and face were accentuated by strands of nearly white hair.

"I should have come to see you long ago," said Carina, glancing at the girl who still did not rise from the fire.

Oriana spoke to the girl, "Angela, come and meet Carina. Carina was the countess married to Count Giancarlo. She left Nice to go back to her people when he was killed."

The girl rose from the fireplace and came mincingly toward them. Carina read fear in her eyes. She felt a strong urge to comfort her. The girl was young, perhaps thirteen, but seemed totally lacking in self confidence. Carina saw how she stayed close to Oriana, raising her eyes only briefly to give her a suspicious glance. Of average height, the girl's hair was auburn, like her own, and her skin pale. Her figure seemed already womanly under her loose garment, but her demeanor and bowed posture gave her a forlorn appearance.

"Don't be afraid," said Oriana. "Carina is the last person who would ever hurt you.

The girl still seemed fearful, and Carina impulsively stepped forward to give the waiflike creature a hug. The girl went stiff at her embrace. Carina moved back, surprised at her manner.

"She has had a very difficult life," said Oriana. "From what I have been able to find out, her parents were killed a long time ago. She has subsisted since then as a hanger on. Oriana came closer to Carina and spoke confidentially. "I think she has been raped. Maybe repeatedly. She won't even look at a man. She trusts no one and has had so little care. Even talking is difficult with her." Oriana continued. "One of our knights, while riding with his daughter, found her outside the city. The girl was able to coax her to enter the protection of the town walls, and the knight tried to find someone who would care for her. That was two weeks ago. I took her in, and am teaching her the healing arts. She has much to learn, but she is smart."

Carina looked again at the poor girl and her heart went out to her. Her own problem suddenly seemed small in comparison. Yet, her problem was important—very important.

"Oriana, I need to get your advice about a personal problem. Can I talk with you alone?"

"We can walk together and speak in the courtyard." Taking a shawl off a hook on the wall, she put it over her shoulders and told the girl, "Angela, I'll be back before long. Don't let the fire get too hot. The cauldron should only simmer, not bubble."

They went along the hall and then downstairs and out into the courtyard. Dusk was falling, giving the few people outdoors a shadowy appearance. Carina and Oriana walked together at an unhurried pace.

"It's about me, Oriana. Married over a year and a half and still no stirring inside. I am so disappointed. I know Uberto is too, but he says nothing. It is what he doesn't say that makes me feel bad. He no longer talks of children, of having a son or two he can train to become knights. Or of a daughter who will be like me."

"A year and a half is not so long," said Oriana, reassuringly. "It can take longer."

"Or it can be never," said Carina, bowing her head.

"Have you done anything so far?"

"Yes. Father Carlo has blessed my womb. I felt sure afterwards I was with child, but I was only late."

"I see," said the older woman thoughtfully. "Nothing else?"

"I tried nettle leaf. One of the midwives said it would help me to conceive.

"Yes, that is usually a good herb to use. Carina, I need to ask you a personal question. I hope you will not be offended."

Carina looked around the courtyard, making sure there was no one close enough to hear. "What is it, Oriana? If it will help us, I don't care."

"When a man and a woman are together, it is much easier for a woman to conceive if she too has enjoyment. If a woman holds back or cannot be at ease, children don't come as readily."

Carina looked around again before answering. "Are you saying a woman should like the joining? I had not heard that before."

"To increase the chance of conceiving, yes. Hardly anyone else will tell you this."

Once again Carina checked to make sure no one was near. Then, speaking close to Oriana's ear she whispered, "I like it." Immediately, her face reddened and she felt she had revealed far too much.

"Well, then that is not the problem. Carina, no priest or sage will tell you this, but your empty womb can also be a problem with the man."

"That I find hard to believe, especially in regard to Uberto."

"Still, it is possible. There are many things we do not fully understand. I will be forthright with you, Carina. With the exception of giving you a potion, there is little I can do for you. I think you should talk to Patrizio."

"You mean Giancarlo's other son? The one I have scarcely seen?"

"He has more knowledge than anyone else."

"I don't know, Oriana. A priest is one thing, but to talk to an ordinary man about it, even if he is a count. . ."

"He is not ordinary," Oriana broke in. "Not at all. He hardly seems to have feelings at all. He probably does, but he keeps them well hidden. In truth, he is rather unnerving—his eyes especially. But he has never hurt anyone."

9

They arrived back at Oriana's door. Carina went inside to get the potion. She listened to Oriana's directions on how it should be used. She thanked her, and now on the other side of her door she hesitated. The healer had told her which apartment was Patrizio's. Carina was not sure she wanted to go to him. She returned to her own suite, hoping to find Uberto there. He still had not returned. Impulsively, she decided to visit Patrizio.

As she made her way to his quarters, she felt uneasy. At the very least, she should have told Uberto. For a woman to visit a man was always suspect. Oriana had told her to, however, and she would know if there was any risk. Besides, Carina knew it would be hard for her to talk to Uberto about what she was doing. Uberto's thinking was different from hers. He wanted to leave things in God's hands. He believed in prayer, but not in doing other things which to him seemed unnatural. She had to keep her thoughts to herself at least for a time. Only afterward, if successful, would she tell Uberto.

She knocked on Patrizio's door, glad there was no one around to see her.

"Who is it," came a deep voice from within.

"Carina," she answered, her head close to the door so she didn't need to raise her voice any louder than necessary.

"Carina, come in," he answered, his voice sounding as if he were just on the other side.

She heard a bolt being withdrawn, and after opening the door, he stood in front of her. Carina entered and then stood looking at him. Glowing candles illuminated his eyes, which seemed to look though her. Moreover, the resemblance to his father, Giancarlo, was uncanny. Like him, he wore all black, with dark hair, and though not quite as robust, he stood taller than his father.

Carina was confused, and was not sure she wanted to confide in this man. Patrizio seemed to look at her for an inordinately long time until he finally said, "Everyone says I look much like my father."

Not wanting to stare at him, Carina's eyes roved the apartment. She realized he had obviously read her consternation at the strong resemblance. She took courage and looking up to face him, stated her purpose. "I have been talking to Oriana. She said you have wisdom about many things. She thought you might help me."

"I don't know if I can. Oriana seems to have more faith in me than I do. I study nature and pursue understanding. But I am not a healer. Sit down, Carina."

Carina did as he said, though her faith in anything he could do was rapidly diminishing. She sensed Patrizio was a different man than his father. She looked again at the apartment and saw that there were a number of strange looking instruments about. Three of them were clustered beneath a larger than usual window. The apartment itself was sparsely furnished except for bookcases. There were more books there than she had ever before seen in one place.

He sat down across the table from her. Carina was still unresolved as to whether she wanted to talk to Patrizio about her problem. The silence was becoming awkward, especially as she more than once caught him looking at her in his intense way. Did she perhaps remind him of someone?

"I don't know if I should be here," she said finally, glancing toward the door. "You said you are not a healer. I don't know if I have a sickness, but there is something wrong with me."

"Whatever it is, you don't need to tell me, Carina. I have much yet to learn and though I would like to be able to help you, it may be unlikely that I can. I know you suffered at your father's and my father's deaths. We have shared a common sorrow. Now you have Uberto. I hope your union with him has helped you to forget your grief."

"Oh, yes, yes," spoke Carina spontaneously. "Uberto has been good to me."

Patrizio's eyes had been downcast, but he looked up at her when he heard the evident cheer in her voice. "I'm glad for you."

Carina noted Patrizio's words were spoken sincerely, but with a measure of sadness. For some unknown reason, she at that moment felt she could confide in him. Placing one hand on the table in front of her, she said, "the only barrier to our happiness is my empty womb." There, she had said it, and she looked to Patrizio for his response.

Patrizio looked away from her. He seemed embarrassed. He coughed and then turned back toward her. Carina was glad he didn't smile, or worse, laugh at her.

"People do come to me. At times, I am able to help them. Often not. Your situation, you have done the usual things?"

Carina lowered her eyes from his gaze. She murmured, "Yes."

"I heard you were married soon after the expedition came back from defeating the Saracens at Tours."

"Yes."

"It is a relatively long time to be without child. Yet there is still a chance that if you wait you will yet conceive."

Carina sighed. "So I have been told. There is still a chance. Life goes on around me, but nothing happens. Peasant wives conceive it seems on their first night. I look at them and their joy at their bouncing babies at their breast. I turn away in sadness. People look at me wondering what is the matter with me. They even slyly make fun of Uberto. I see these things, I am not blind with no hearing. It is a curse to be barren."

Carina's head was bowed, and she didn't notice Patrizio rise from his chair. She felt his hand on her shoulder, and with teary eyes she turned to face him.

"There are some who called me learned, Carina. Most of what I know has come from these tomes. With a hand still on her shoulder, he indicated with his other all the shelves filled with books. I believe little in magic, as it is commonly practiced with spells and divinations. Yet there remain some things best described as mystical that cannot be understood in a natural way. Our religion speaks of many of these. I am sure you have prayed to have a child, thus far to no avail. If you are willing, and have the means to pursue it, there is a more powerful mystery that can give you what you want."

Carina rose from the chair trembling. She could hardly believe her ears. She stood looking into Patrizio's calm eyes and saw no trace of anything other than sincerity. "What, what did you, say," she stammered.

"There is a way, a power beyond anything we know."

"Tell me," she said impatiently, still hardly able to believe what she was hearing. "What is it?"

"The one true cross. The cross on which Our Lord was crucified."

Carina sat down again, weak with strong, conflicting emotions. Wouldn't it be a sin, she wondered, to use the cross for her own personal need? On the other hand, where could she ever find it? She didn't know what to say to Patrizio. Finally she remembered what she had learned. "But the cross, if anything remains of it, isn't it in Jerusalem? How could anyone go there? It is controlled by the Saracens."

"An incorrect assumption," spoke Patrizio from across the room, where he stood before one of his book cases. It is historically very clear that in 327 AD large pieces of the cross were moved from Jerusalem to Rome by St. Helena, the mother of Constantine.

"How did she know she found the true cross? Didn't the Romans crucify many people?" she asked.

"St. Helena found three crosses, buried under a pagan temple built over the tomb of Christ. Not knowing

14

which of the three was the true cross, she and her assistants found a woman near death. She touched two of the crosses and nothing happened. When the third was touched to her, the woman rose from her bed, completely healed."

"So, the cross is in Rome," Carina concluded.

"Not only there," answered Patrizio as he continued to look on the shelves for the book he was after. At last he pulled out a dusty volume. "Pieces of it were distributed throughout much of the Roman territory before the Empire was destroyed."

He brought a book to the table and leafed through the pages. Bound in parchment, it had a musty odor. "Here it is," said Patrizio. He pointed to a line of handwritten Latin that had been underlined. "I am fortunate to have this volume."

Carina bent down to look where he pointed. She tried to read the sentence. "The . . . earth is full of the . . . of the cross of Christ," she made out.

"You have it. 'The whole earth is full of the relics of the cross of Christ.' Do you know when that was written?"

Carina lifted a hand in a gesture to show she had no idea.

"In AD 348, by Cyril of Jerusalem. It is apparent that everybody wanted a piece of it. At the time, when Rome was struggling to fight the increasing invasions, some well off Christians even carried a splinter of the wood encased in gold or silver around their necks to ward off evil."

"Wonderful," said Carina, concern easing from her countenance. Then it shouldn't be difficult to find a piece. That's all I need, don't you think, just a piece of it?"

"It is possible the smallest fragment would have just as much power as a larger one. However, it may not be easy to find a true piece of the cross. You can well imagine that much common wood was hawked for genuine to make a profit."

"How could anyone tell if a piece was real or just an ordinary piece of wood?"

"The large piece of the cross they have in Rome is real, there is no doubt. A major monastery or Cathedral, especially if it has somehow preserved its gold and silver crucifixes from the barbarians, might still have a part of the real cross, though it may be sealed inside a crucifix. Since so many hundreds of years have passed, the only certain way to know is if a fragment of the wood heals."

Carina sighed. "I don't know where to begin. I definitely don't want to steal crucifixes and then melt them down to see if there is wood inside."

"From the little I have read on the subject, often the wood was placed within a hollow opening and then sealed with wax."

"I don't know, Patrizio, this whole thing is beginning to sound too complicated. I wonder if it is right to be thinking of doing this. Especially, taking a crucifix from a church. What would Father Carlo or the bishop say if they heard of it?"

"True, they might not understand. On the other hand, you would need only a sliver."

16

"Even if I were able to obtain a piece, I don't know how to use it. Just touch it and that's all?"

"It is probably important to pray as well, but since no one can be sure it is you and not Uberto, you both should, at the very least, touch the wood. My recommendation would be to burn it in your room at night, so you both inhale its essence."

"I see," said Carina, a picture forming in her head. "I would use it like incense. Unfortunately, when the piece is destroyed no one else would be able to benefit from it." She looked up at Patrizio who stood near where she was seated.

"You only need the tiniest sliver, Carina," he reminded her. "Besides, you could keep the ashes in a safe place. Maybe even the ashes will retain power."

Carina remained sitting, thoughtful. The room was growing dark, and Patrizio lit another candle. He did not rush her and she was glad of that. She would do nearly anything to be able to give Uberto a son or daughter. Unless their desire for children was somehow not meant to be. She stood up and went to Patrizio who was a few steps away. Reaching for his hand, she squeezed it in both of hers and thanked him. Standing so close, she couldn't help but notice his dark eyes that seemed fixed on her. She turned to leave and he moved past her to open the door. Again, she thanked him, and exiting, walked slowly and thoughtfully toward her room.

Uberto wasn't there. Hungry, she went to look for him in the hall. He was there with his friends, Guy and Wotano, and one of them had just said something that caused them all to laugh. Uberto saw her coming, and standing up, invited her to join them. Carina was very much inclined to talk to him about what she had learned from Patrizio, but certainly when he was with friends was not the time to do it.

"You go ahead with what you are talking about," she said. She noted Uberto gave her a curious look before the three resumed their conversation. He had gotten good at reading her, and probably knew she had something on her mind. It could wait; she would see him soon in their room. She helped herself to the food on the tables. Not seeing any of her family, she joined two peasant women who had also made the trip from her domain.

Before long, she saw Uberto coming toward her, and turning, she caught sight of Guy and Wotano leaving. Uberto took a seat next to her, put an arm around her waist, and eyed her with interest. "You have something to tell me, I can tell."

Carina swallowed the piece of food in her mouth. "Wait until we get back to our room." The two peasant women at her sided bowed their heads momentarily in deference to Uberto, a knight. Carina continued to chat with them for a short time until she finished eating. Then she and Uberto walked together to their chamber where a single candle provided the only light.

They were alone, and Uberto put his arms around her as they stood face to face. Carina looked into his eyes.

"What do you have hidden behind those devious, enchanting eyes that cannot be told in public?" he asked.

Carina delighted in his strong, encircling arms that were pulling her tighter to him. Yet she knew she would have to choose her words carefully. Perhaps it was better to wait.

"When you hold me so close I hardly know what to say." She enjoyed the feel of his hands moving over her body.

"How fetchingly beautiful you were this afternoon when I saw how the water made your tunic cling to your figure. And your hair, hanging down and gleaming like burnished gold in the sun. I wanted to take you there on the beach."

Carina knew it was not the time for talking about serious things. From behind her back, she reached a hand to the door, making sure it was locked. Then, looking saucily into Uberto's eyes she said, "Do with me what you will, my prince."

Chapter Two

Carina and Uberto slept well, and did not hear the secret movement of soldiers in the night. The guards and others had, however. Under cover of darkness, men had been heard, rather than seen, disembarking from a large ship and then moving to the east. By morning's light, everyone had learned of it. Yet so much was not known. How many? Had others come before them? Would others come later? Nor did anyone know their mission, but everyone feared the worst. Unfortunately, it was the same day that Carina and all those who had gone to Nice were to return to her manor.

That same morning, young Count Leonardo, heir of his deceased father, Count Giancarlo, sent twenty-five additional knights to join the ranks of those cautiously returning through the forest to their manor. Leonardo would have liked to send more, but the defense of his city, the walled town of Nice, was his primary concern. As they traveled, Carina saw Uberto with Renzo at the head of the column, and knew that Corrado, her father's most trusted military advisor, was also nearby. He appeared ahead just now, a husky, short man with cropped gray hair, whose movements were quick and powerful despite his age. She knew that further ahead were scouts, whose job was to make sure the enemy did not lay a trap for them.

They stopped for lunch, posting guards as a precaution. Still far away from their destination, the soldiers and all those with them relaxed a bit in the warm sun of the clearing.

Afterwards, they traveled through the day at a leisurely pace until finally Carina was glad to see the territory near her manor coming into view. There had been no incidents as they journeyed through the forest and she was looking forward to seeing her brother Amadeo, Gertrude and others. Amadeo had not joined them in their travel to Nice because of his crippled leg. Gertrude's fear of horses had kept her from going. Carina's thoughts were suddenly interrupted as two swift riding scouts pulled up directly in front of Renzo. Though they spoke quietly, Carina caught the urgency in their voices. She saw the shocked look on Renzo and Corrado's face. Something was terribly wrong.

She watched as the two hastily whispered directions to the knights. Finally, her brother Renzo spoke to them all in a hushed voice. "My people, the Saracens have overpowered our defenses and taken control of our fortress. All the women and children must go quickly back to the safety of Nice. Go with the knights on my right. The rest of us will remain here to protect against an enemy pursuit. Then we will follow you back to Nice."

Carina saw the determined and resigned look on her brother's face, and on Uberto's. Uberto rode to her, and still on horseback, she hugged him with all her strength and kissed him goodbye. She well knew the danger he faced.

"I will come back to you," he said, "if I have to crawl on my hands and knees through the forest. Wait for me."

"I will wait for you forever." They kissed again and then she lifted her hand toward him in a final farewell as he rode away to join the others.

"Alright," said Donato, one of a handful of knights assigned to lead over thirty women and children back. "We must return in all haste back to Nice. Our very lives may depend on our speed. Let's be off!"

Carina took her sister-in-law's baby, so Antonia could keep up the pace while riding with her four year old son. She looped her carrying bag over her neck and shoulders. The two women exchanged anxious glances. Both their husbands had stayed behind to fight.

Once they were away from the women and children, Uberto learned the full tragedy of the Saracen conquest. At the fortress of the manor, five poles stood over the ramparts and on each of them was the pierced helmet of a knight. What was worse, for the thirty-two men who readied themselves against an attack, they had been seen. As Renzo moved his force into a defensive position hidden by trees and shrubbery, already they could hear the battle cries of Saracens pouring through the raised gate.

Too many to fight, thought Uberto.

Renzo must have thought so too, for when the enemy advanced he called for a retreat. Not along the trail, that would have led them to the women and children, but through the forest. Their route through the woods was not easy going. The horses at times resisted and the men were whiplashed by trees and bushes. The Saracens followed behind, and seemed to be gaining on them. Uberto looked back and estimated they were double their number. For over two hours they continued moving through the trackless forest with the enemy immediately behind. Then they came to a hill that rose over a steep bluff. Riding up the side of the hill, they waited at the top for the enemy, expecting to use the height to their advantage. They didn't know the Saracens had archers.

Just in time, they saw bowmen bending to notch their arrows. Renzo again called a retreat. They began hurrying down the other side of the hill, but the Saracen horsemen were already attacking. Fighting alongside his friends Guy and Wotano, Uberto faced the forward onslaught of their cavalry. He had not yet reached the peak of the hill, and was unable to turn his horse around in time to retreat. He struck at the first two Saracens to reach him, impaling one on his sword, and then striking at the other with the butt of his weapon. A sword he didn't see struck him on the head, cutting through his hard leather helmet. He felt a sharp stab of pain and fell dizzily to the ground, where he remained, to all appearances dead. He could not have known what happened next. Another of Renzo's men was struck down beside him, and the rest of the small force retreated beyond the hill into the forest.

Much later, Uberto awakened. Everything was quiet except for the twitter of nearby birds. His head ached with a terrible, constant pounding. Weak and nauseous, he didn't know if he had the strength to move. He attempted to move the fingers of the hand under his chest. He was satisfied to know they worked. He tried to move his other arm, lying splayed out behind his shoulder where he couldn't see. His fingers were numb. His whole arm was numb. Dizzy, he didn't know if he could stand up. He tried rolling over and managed to do so. A fresh wave of nausea overwhelmed him. He vomited, moving his head in time so it came out the side of his mouth onto the ground. He lay motionless, too weak to move. Sleep came over him.

* * *

Carina awoke at dawn from a fitful sleep. Gradually the town came to life and she heard voices and footsteps in the street and wagon wheels rolling. Dressing quickly, she went downstairs and then outside looking for anyone who could tell her news. Those she asked had heard nothing, and she went to the gate where she saw Heida, Guy's wife. She carried her young daughter in her arms.

"Have you heard anything?" she asked her.

"No, nothing. No one has heard anything." The woman looked up at Carina and then down at the ground.

Carina felt her dejection, and she went to her side. Speaking with an assurance she didn't feel, she added, "They will come back to us, probably later today." Heida turned to her and the two women embraced.

Changing the subject Carina asked, "How many months is your little one now?"

"Already almost a year, and she is so active. Guy is proud."

Carina noted that for a brief moment Heida forgot her husband's plight in thinking about her baby—until she mentioned his name. The women hugged again, and Carina left, not knowing how she would pass the time in waiting. Had she been at her own manor she would have returned to her loom. It was better than doing nothing. She walked the short distance toward the center of town and saw the cathedral. Bowing her head, she headed for it, not knowing if on a weekday morning it was open. She went in, and kneeling down, prayed for the return of the knights. Especially for Uberto and her brother.

Chapter Three

Daylight, and a bug crawling across his face awakened Uberto. He was no longer nauseous, and the throbbing of his head had lessened. He felt weak and very thirsty, and for that reason more than any other he felt the need to get up. He moved each of his limbs one at a time to make sure his body was whole. Then, pulling his knees up, he tried to get up on his hands and knees. He wobbled unsteadily before falling to his side.

He was hungry. He didn't know if his weakness was due to hunger or to injury. He had been in a battle, but strangely, he could barely remember it. Who had he been fighting and why had he been left behind—left for dead? He was conscious of wearing military garb and he could see an insignia on his tunic. He did not know its meaning. He was able to sit up, though even that seemed to tire him. He tried to remember what happened. Suddenly, he realized he did not know anything about himself. The only memories that came to him were those of his youth.

Especially of when his family was attacked and his sister raped. Not happy memories.

Driven by thirst and hunger, he tried to get up again. The throbbing in his head grew worse at his exertion. Finally, he managed to get to his feet. Dizzily, he looked around, and beginning to swoon, he grasped a small tree to steady himself. He scrutinized the forest, trying to determine which direction to go. Nothing looked familiar to him. Then, lying in deep grass, he saw a body. He went to it. The man was sprawled out unnaturally. Uberto saw that he wore the same insignia. One of his countrymen, from whatever country it was. Uberto didn't recognize him. The stench of death emanated from the man. Uberto turned away, sickened.

He had to find water. Already his lips were dry and his mouth parched. Anything, anything to drink. He looked upwards at the tree branches, hoping there would be some fruit he could savor. Not seeing any, he began laboriously trudging, one foot over the other, his head pounding. He lifted a hand to touch his scalp and found a mound of hair matted no doubt with blood. Even touching his hair near the wound caused a stabbing pain. He staggered onward, seeking a downward course in hope of finding a stream.

He realized he had no sword. Probably it had been taken. He felt a small knife in a holster still at his side under his tunic. The thought of killing an animal for food came to him and faded away. He would need quickness. Quickness that he didn't have.

Heavy footed, his head throbbing, he tromped along the grass between a hill on his right and the forest on his left. He didn't know how long he could continue. His eyes caught sight of the red fruit of a lone raspberry bush, and he laboriously knelt down beside it, picking it clean of the few berries not already eaten by birds. Getting up again onto his feet exhausted the little energy he had. He would have lain down again but knew he might not get up. He had to find water.

The day wore on. Uberto still was moving slowly and unsteadily along the edge of the unknown forest, holding onto trees, then moving on, hoping to find water or someone who could give him food and shelter for the night. Finally, as the sun was beginning to go down in the sky, he heard ahead what sounded like a small stream coursing along the meadow. To his right was a steep hill looming in the distance that no doubt fed a watercourse. He stumbled ahead until he came to the water where he buckled, head extended over the tiny stream. Bending his face into the clear, narrow rivulet, he drank deeply, pausing only for air.

Thirst quenched for the moment, he remained lying on the ground with scarcely enough energy to back away from the water. He raised his head to look around, not bothering to rise from his prone position. A short distance to the right he saw a circle of rocks lying at the edge of the water. He wondered if there were people living in the area. Night was already beginning to fall, and he knew he didn't have the strength to go on. Backing away from the water on his hands and knees, he saw a clump of tall grass. There he would rest. Maybe the constant ache of his head would subside if he could get some sleep. He glanced again toward the circle of rocks, where he saw some movement. It was a woman, one with hair of golden yellow looking at him. Believing himself to be dreaming, somehow the image of her face stayed with him. Small comfort as he drifted to sleep.

Talia saw the stranger and was afraid. She hid from his line of sight in a place where she could still glimpse him through the reeds. When instead of standing up he backed away from the water, she knew he was sick. Still, he might be dangerous. Torn between wanting to help him and fear, she looked in his direction as she filled her jar with water. Putting it on her head, she held it there with one hand while returning quickly along the path that led a short distance to her stronghold.

In the morning, she returned along the path, this time with her younger sister, the manor blacksmith, and a cart. She carried a knife and he carried a sword. The young girl stood back as Talia led the blacksmith to where she had last seen him. He was still there. She watched him sleeping, with his hands under his head for a pillow. Leaving the ironsmith, she came closer. Cautiously, she came near, and hand extended, she pushed him on the shoulder, and then backed away quickly.

Uberto wakened at her touch, and looking up, saw the girl whose face he remembered from the night before. Squinting at her in the sunlight, he realized she was not just a dream. Standing two paces away, she looked down at him, her eyes wide with concern. Her bright hair hung long, well past her shoulders, and her mouth was set as if she waited for a response. Uberto also saw the man behind her holding the sword. Not tall, but husky, he leaned forward, eyes fixed on him, hair balding in front.

The girl spoke. "Are you not well? Do you need help?"

Uberto tried to rise, lifting himself first on one knee. He willed to be strong, as he didn't wish to need assistance, but when he tried to rise, he fell down. He was weaker than he realized. The girl went to him and put her hands on his shoulders. The blacksmith brought the cart, and taking his arms and legs, the two of them lifted him into it. Uberto felt a keen sense of embarrassment at not being able to help himself. For a time he looked backward as they wheeled him along a trail through the forest before falling asleep again.

He wakened confused, in a bed. He found himself in a room within an unfamiliar house. His head still ached, though not as badly as before. Under the blanket, his hand touched his body. He was naked. Someone had removed all his clothing. He still felt weak and terribly hungry and thirsty. A soft repetitive sound came from another room. It sounded like a spinning wheel. He wanted to get up to find some food. Where had they put his clothes?

Talia rose frequently from her spinning to go to the next room and look at the stranger who lay on her sister's bed in the room. With the smith's help she had removed his clothing and sponge bathed him, glad that except for two healed scars he had no other injuries except his head.

She noted the firm muscles of his body and the emblem on his tunic that likely meant he was a knight. From where, she did not know. Only the matted clump of blood in his hair she did not touch. She was drawn to the gentle repose of his face, and she knew she should not look at him long for he probably belonged to another. She wished he would waken. He needed to eat to regain his strength.

"Aaaah," he uttered, lifting his arms from his sides.

Hearing his voice, she entered the room. She came closer, and standing over him saw his eyes open. He shuddered, and his eyes seemed to survey the room. Then they looked up to her and their eyes locked. Talia looked away, suddenly feeling flustered by something she could not explain.

Turning back to him she said, "I am glad you are finally awake," she said.

"I feel as though I have been asleep for a long time." Uberto closed his eyes. When he opened them, the woman was still there. She was not a dream. She still stood over him, her long, blond hair hanging down in front as she leaned toward him. Her tunic was simple and looked freshly cleaned with a small adornment woven above her heart. Its loose folds did not hide her figure and he saw that her smile was touched with concern. He did not feel his usual strength, but for the first time his head did not cause him distressing pain

"How do you feel," she asked, taking a step closer to the bed. .

"Much better, though I feel weak and very hungry." He grabbed the corner of the blanket covering him and with one hand and tossed it aside, then remembered, he had nothing on.

"You don't want to do that," said the girl, turning away from looking at him.

"Where are my clothes?" Uberto tried to speak loudly, but he quickly realized that even his voice sounded weak. He retrieved the blanket. "Did you take them?" The girl was still turned away from him.

"Are you covered?" she asked. She turned back to him, a hint of a smile registering on her face. "Yes, it was my uncle and I who undressed you and washed you. You were very sick, though today your color has improved. Your clothes are washed too; I will go and get them."

Uberto didn't like the thought of being undressed and washed by strangers—particularly a young woman he didn't know. However, there was nothing he could do about it now. He wanted to get up, to test his strength, and most of all to get something to eat. He was ravenously hungry.

She came back carrying his clothes and unceremoniously dropped them on the bed. "There," she said. "You seem strong enough to get them on yourself, but call if you need help. I'll be nearby." Turning back at the doorway she said, "Be careful, you may still be faint. When you are dressed you can come and get some food."

Uberto watched her as she left the room. She was pretty as well as kind. Had she not been, he might be dead now. Immediately he began putting on his clothes. He felt weak, breathing harder than he would have thought from such activity. Once dressed, he sat down on the bed and rested a moment before getting up and unsteadily walking out of the room. The throbbing of his head started again, though not as bad as before. Holding onto the doorway, he found the girl in the next room bending over a pot hanging over a fireplace. The aroma of its contents made his mouth water.

"How do you feel," she asked, glancing away from the pot to look at him.

"Weaker than I thought but very hungry. Whatever you are cooking has an excellent aroma."

She left the pot to go to him, and taking his arm led him forward to a chair at the table. "Sit down. I'm afraid if you don't you will fall. Are you sure you shouldn't be back in bed? I could bring your food there." She seemed to take a good look at him before going back to where the kettle simmered on the hearth.

"I'll be all right once I get some food in my stomach."

"No you won't be just yet. It's going to take some time." She went to the pot and ladled the stew into a bowl, then added a sprinkle of some condiment before bringing it to him.

His eyes followed her. "What was that you put into the bowl?

"Some spice," she said with a smile as she set the steaming bowl in front of him. She watched him take the spoon and eat ravenously, not even looking up until he was done. She quickly got him a large cup of mead and watched as he downed it, only once stopping for air.

"Do you have more?"

"You should wait awhile. Your stomach needs time to get used to eating a full meal again. How do you feel?"

"Better.

Despite his remaining hunger, Uberto knew she was right. He still felt weak, and even eating seemed to tire his body. He fought the desire to return to the bed, thinking it was unseemly for a knight to sleep at midday. He leaned back against his chair and took a long look at the woman. She had been watching him as she continued her spinning. At his stare, she turned away. He studied her features. Pale skin accentuated by her hair that fell in ringlets at her shoulders, intense dark eyes that looked away if she found him observing her, a feminine figure not hidden by the clean, light colored decorated tunic she wore. Momentarily, another thought came to him, a thought of another woman, but it quickly vanished.

Confused, he continued to sit at the table trying to remember how he was injured and what happened before. Try as he might, nothing came to him. He put his hand to the knot on his head. He could not remember the blow. What had he been doing when he was injured? And before that, what of his life? Suddenly dazed by the emptiness of his thoughts, he desperately tried to think about his past. Nothing came to him except his youth. That he could remember, and he winced as he recalled the attack that left his mother, father and sister dead. He was a grown man now, what had happened in all those years since childhood? He shook his head in an effort to recall, and sadly realized he knew nothing of himself, not evening knowing if he had a wife or had even known a woman. He dropped his head and a silent tear ran down his cheek.

A new thought came to him. Turning to the woman he asked, "Was there anything else I had in my possession when you found me?"

She returned his gaze and for a moment seemed undecided before answering, "Yes, you had a dagger and an emblem attached to your outer tunic which I removed before washing your garments."

"I need them," he said, trying to suppress his excitement, for he knew they might tell him something about himself.

"They can wait. What you really need is to get back in bed. I can see how weak you are."

Uberto knew she was right about his condition, but he needed to grab hold of his life. Summoning his strength, he said to her in the loudest voice he could muster, "I will see them before returning to bed!"

Uberto saw her look uncertainly at him and then she left her spinning to go to the fireplace. Behind a stack of wood near the hearth, she picked up a knife and an emblem and brought them to him. "Here," she said, eyeing him closely.

Uberto looked intently at the knife, noticing how well it was made, and at the half circle design on the hilt with lines radiating from it, obviously a depiction of the rising sun. With a peculiar joy, he looked down at his own breast, and there, over his heart was the same symbol woven into his garment. He realized with a certain awe that he was a knight, belonging thereby to a fortified manor. He looked up at the girl.

"It is well made," she said.

Uberto didn't want to tell her that he could not even remember his lord or where his fortress was located. He wanted to rest now, content for now that he had at least established an important part of his own identity. His hope was that one day soon he would awaken and be able to fill in the huge emptiness that remained.

"Thank you," he said to her. "I needed to see that you have them. A man without a weapon is defenseless. Would that I also had my sword. Thank you for all you have done for me. You are right. I am very tired and will lay down for a while."

Chapter Four

Carina was in her room when she heard the noise and excitement in the courtyard. The men were returning! She rushed downstairs, out the door and across the open space along the wide thoroughfare where already a crowd was gathering. She jostled her way to be near the front so she could see, as the gate was raised, Uberto and the other men on horseback filing in. Rising up around her were the cries of joy of women who saw their son or husband returning safely. Still, she didn't see Uberto, and her heart pounded with fear as the last of the knights went through the gates. Desperately she sought out someone who would know his fate. She saw Guy, already getting down from his horse to receive the joyful embrace of his wife. Carina interrupted them, asking loudly, "Where is Uberto!"

Guy looked up from holding his wife and then separated himself from her to face Carina. "I'm sorry," he said with downcast eyes. "He didn't make it."

"What do you mean?" came her flat, guttural response as she moved close to confront him.

"I'm sorry," he repeated. "I was next to him when they attacked. He was closest to the enemy when we were overwhelmed. He went down, struck by a sword. Hagan also was struck down. Uberto's valor helped the rest of us to escape over the hill."

"Are you sure he was dead?" she asked in a voice so strained it was hard to understand.

"What?"

"Was he dead? Are you sure?" She put her hand impulsively on Guy's shoulder as she pleaded to know more of Uberto.

"I cannot say for sure. We had to rush away or be slaughtered."

Carina turned away from him, her head bowed as she walked without feeling to her room. Sitting on her bed, a flood of tears poured down her cheeks. It was all she could do not to scream. There was a knock on the door. Quickly drying her eyes she said, "Who is it?"

"Your brother."

"Come in."

Renzo entered, his eyes downcast. He sat down beside her on the bed. They embraced. "I'm sorry, Carina."

Carina didn't look up nor did she even look at her brother, but she continued to hold him, her body

38

quivering with emotion. Then she looked directly at him. "Did you see what happened?"

"Only a glimpse from afar. I saw a glint of steel near his head and then he fell to the ground. Nothing more. He was in the rear guard defending our escape up the hill. Because of him and two others holding them off, we were able to escape. He is a true hero, Carina."

"But do you know for sure that he was killed?" Her eyes fixed on those of her brother

"We were retreating, Carina, or we all would have been killed. Yes, it is possible he could have survived and the enemy did not finish him off if he lived. Possible, but to be honest with you, very unlikely."

"Thank you, brother," she managed a bittersweet smile. "It is better to know what happened than not. If anyone could survive it would be him."

Renzo got up and Carina stood as well. They embraced once again, without words, and he left her.

Carina remained in the room, not bothering to light a candle as darkness descended. Much later, there was another knock on her door. It was her sister-in-law, Antonia.

"Are you alright? I can't even see you. Do you mind if I light a candle from the hall sconce?"

Carina said nothing. Antonia took her sconce and quickly returned, having lit the candle. She surveyed Carina who still sat with bowed head on the bed. "I bet you haven't had anything to eat, have you?"

Carina shook her head in reply, scarcely looking up.

Antonia cocked her head and then went immediately to Carina, throwing her arms around her. "I'm sorry, Carina."

Carina tightly held onto her sister-in-law, allowing her tears to once again flow freely. "I don't know what I'm going to do, Antonia. I have no desire to live anymore."

"Carina, don't say that. You are young with a full life ahead of you. I know how terrible you must feel. You need a time of mourning until you can get over your loss. Everyone understands. Pray to be strong. Join Renzo and I and the children in our chamber some evenings, whenever you feel like it. We can play some music and sing. The children love you, you know that."

"I know, I love them too, and you, Antonia," she said, taking her hands in hers. "Maybe I will someday get over this, but I don't know how. Uberto was so good to me even when I could not give him a child." She lowered her head while still holding Antonia's hands, the tears coming again. "I'm sorry, Antonia. You see how wrought up I am. Just thinking of him and I'm in tears."

"It's alright, Carina," said Antonia, embracing her again. "It's going to take time before you can begin to overcome your loss. Don't worry about it and don't try to hold back your feelings."

She left. Carina remembered what Antonia had told her after her father and Giancarlo had died. Even though it was late, she decided to ride. She went to the stable and readied her horse, Callista. Just as had happened the last time, she was stopped at the gate, but when they saw it was she, the guards finally raised it. She quietly walked Callista down the hill, consciously enjoying the scent of her favorite animal. Once she was on level ground, she mounted and rode, not too swiftly, as the night was lit only by a half moon and she feared her horse might stumble. As always, she felt good to be in the saddle, with the breeze whipping around her. With Callista she was in control, something she seemed to have very little of anymore. She slowed down and walked her horse, heading toward the beach.

By the light of the moon, she saw the waves of the Mediterranean splash on the shore, their crests tipped with foam. She rode along the coast, smelling its clean freshness, not knowing how far she was going or when she would turn back. Suddenly a rider came from behind a hill, causing her heart to jump at the danger in his sudden appearance. Not waiting to see who it could be, she immediately turned around, ready to race to the safety of the town walls.

"Carina," the voice came from the stranger.

Surprised that he would know her name, she turned her head. "Who are you?"

"Patrizio."

"Patrizio. What are you doing out here?"

"Riding. And you?"

"I can't tell you how much you scared me," she said as he pulled alongside her.

"I was surprised as well to see anyone on my solitary ride. When I saw you were a woman I could guess it might be you."

They rode along together slowly back toward town. In her grief, Carina had nothing further to say, but she felt a certain comfort with Patrizio, especially as he did not try to make conversation. She felt he understood. He was unusual, she realized, and as he continued to say nothing she wondered if she was imagining it or if he really did care. Out of curiosity she said, "You are quiet, Patrizio."

"As are you, my lady. I understand."

"Thank you. People talk to me and say fine things about Uberto, but that doesn't bring him back to me. It is all words, though they are well meaning."

"Words and embraces are all we have to communicate. Sometimes it is not enough."

Carina thought about this as they approached the walls. She wondered about Patrizio. Had he too experienced a loss? They dismounted as they reached the incline to the gate, and she turned to look into his eyes that glowed in the moonlight. Yes, she thought to herself, he too has known pain.

* * *

The next day, Carina felt a new resolve. She could no longer remain in her room doing nothing but thinking about Uberto and feeling sorry for herself. She felt herself energized and didn't know why. The grief was still there, weighing on her, but she realized the need for some meaningful activity in her life. She was a weaver, one who took pride in the fine designs and the excellent garments she was able to make. She went looking for Gina, her spinner.

Inquiring after her, she found that she was staying on the level beneath her and down the hall. She knocked on her door. From within, Gina opened the door slowly. Carina was surprised at her appearance. The girl looked haggard and older than her twenty-two years. "Gina," she exclaimed, "are you alright?"

"Come in," she said, backing away to make room for her.

In the dim light that came through the window, Carina could see across the cluttered room where her two children played. She spontaneously gave Gina a hug. "Oh, Gina, I'm sorry. I had totally forgotten that your husband is also at our fortress, as is my brother."

The two women hugged and then Gina said, "I am so afraid for him, for them all. Why do the knights not mount an expedition to conquer the Saracens there?"

"I don't know, Gina. Surely, they must be planning something. They would not tell us if they are. We will only find out about it after they are gone."

"The waiting is hard. Waiting and not knowing and thinking the worst. But you, my lady. I don't know what to say. I am so sorry."

"Don't say anything, Gina," said Carina, momentarily shrinking back at the thoughts Gina's words brought back. Recovering, she continued with her purpose. "Gina, we have no control over what the men will do, but waiting and doing nothing does neither of us any good. Let's return to our work."

Gina looked up. "Can we? Of course I can always spin, but do you know of a loom you can use?"

"Leave it to me, Gina. I will ask around and find one." The two women said goodbye and Carina exited the room with a certain spring to her step.

That evening in the special room adjacent to Leonardo's suite the leaders met. Leonardo sat on his comfortable chair in the middle of a large, low-lying table which held a roughly drawn picture of a fortress. Occupying the other chairs were Renzo, Heribert, Corrado and Patrizio. Faintly, through the walls, the crying of a baby could be heard, Leonardo's son, but all attention was given to the matter at hand.

The men varied greatly in age, Count Leonardo was youthful and handsome but serious with dark black hair, his older brother Patrizio more slender and taller with piercing dark eyes, and Renzo, still young with a notably friendly demeanor and already a markedly receding hairline. The two older men were Corrado, much older, short with graying hair and a muscular, robust frame, and the leaner Heribert, another experienced member of the old guard who wore the scars of hard fought battles.

"The problem is the peasants," insisted Renzo, accentuating his comment by forceful tapping of his fingers on the table. "The infidels have already killed the knights, and there is no reason they won't kill others."

"Militarily they have little reason to kill them," spoke Corrado, "though they are likely to do it anyway if they won't fight with them against us."

"We cannot simply overwhelm them," said Heribert grimly. "Their force may well be larger than ours and they have the protection of the walls and archers."

"Yes, a full attack is out of the question," agreed Corrado. "In fact, that may be what they want us to do. Then, with our weakened forces they could go on to conquer Nice. I hate to say this, but it might be better not to attack at all."

"They are increasing their manpower there," said Patrizio, in a low, dispassionate voice. "Renzo's domain has little value for them except as a staging ground. Their ultimate goal is to capture Nice."

The men around the table appeared uneasy, and saying nothing, they eyed each other. Renzo was the first to break the silence. "I think you have correctly defined the situation, Patrizio."

Leonardo, since Giancarlo's death in charge of the garrison at Nice, spoke for the first time. "Our objective must be to take back Renzo's domain with as little loss of life as possible. In doing so we will preserve an ally and safeguard Nice. A surprise attack is imperative. Let us each consider by what means we can achieve this outcome and meet here tomorrow at the same time."

Chapter Five

Several days had passed since Uberto had been taken in by Talia with the help of the blacksmith. By this time, he was feeling much better and had even begun to take short rides on a borrowed horse. However, his inability to remember his past continued to disturb him. What kept returning to his consciousness was a feeling, a feeling he was unable to verify, of a bond with a person of particular importance to him. Often, he racked his brain trying to ascertain more, but he simply could not remember. On the other hand, he was becoming aware of a growing feeling for Talia. However, there seemed a mystery about her that he was unable to understand.

She had told him of the tragic circumstances of her family—how her father's stepbrother divided the knights, engineering a coup to take over the estate. Then, the stepbrother murdered her father, and in a supposed hunting accident, also had her brother killed. He wanted his elder son Wagnor to succeed him as lord of the manor.

Talia's mother's health failed after the death of her husband and son, and now, of the family, only Talia and her sister Anna remained. That they were provided for, as deposed royalty, was hardly a consolation. Talia had told him these things almost without rancor, but Uberto had the feeling there was still something else that she didn't say.

Just now, they were riding together on the wide trail leading away from her fortress. He rode Balustead, the horse she had given him—a good stallion but not quite the equal of his own animal. Talia was cheerful, delighting in the sunshine, the flowers, and the landscape, which she enjoyed showing him. Her bright hair caught the rays of the sun and lit up her features, her clear, pale skin, her blue eyes, and the dimple on her chin. At first glance, she gave every appearance of being a carefree maiden. Uberto sensed that down deep there was something in her life that was hidden and troubling. He could see it in her eyes, especially now when their eyes met.

"Let's picnic here," she said, having taken him to a place where they could lean back against a large tree and look out over a wide valley toward a meandering stream. She opened her basket and taking out a large embroidered cloth, spread it over their laps before handing him the larger half of a baguette. They ate companionably, talking about the scenery and the food etc. until they were finished. Then Talia turned to Uberto, and looking him in the eye asked, "You don't have any memory of women, Uberto?" Before he could answer, she snuggled closer, and turning to him put her right hand on his shoulder and quickly kissed him. "No memory of that?" she asked.

Uberto smiled and grabbed her hand so she couldn't get loose. "You know my memory is poor. You're going to have to do it again."

She smiled back at him, and moving so she was close to him, leaned fully into him. Kissing him again, slowly this time, she opened her mouth as his tongue sought entrance. Uberto was fully aware of her breasts rising against his chest, and whether he remembered it or not, he knew what to do. Taking her in his arms, he moved so that his own body clung to hers and he could feel her softness held tight against him.

"Ok!" she said, struggling to be free. "You remember it well, there is no doubt."

Uberto released her, and turned away. The sad thing for him was that he did not remember, or if at all, only vaguely. With bitterness, he said to Talia, "The catch is that I do not remember, but I am not a child so don't play games with me." With some satisfaction he heard her say, "I'm sorry, Uberto."

Uberto was awake late at night on the bed in the extra room. He thought about Talia lying with her sister in the next room. Had she wondered if there was someone else in his life and was her kissing him meant to find out? Did she have feeling for him? She was a beautiful young woman with the bearing of a princess. Strange she was not given to someone. Or was she? No, he thought, for she would not have kissed him.

Uberto wondered about himself. Besides his loss of memory, had his head injury also affected his thinking? He knew after today his passion was unaffected. His desire for a woman was real. Yet was there a faint memory of someone that came to him when he was with Talia? Again, he racked his brain, trying to remember. No picture came to his mind, and frustrated, he finally managed to fall asleep.

The next morning, he again shook his head, maddened by his inability to remember. He had been here for days recuperating, and although strength was coming back to his body, his mind was still blank. Not that he had any difficulty remembering anything since the blow to his head. He noticed sometimes Talia would sprinkle a powder or granules into his food and when he asked about them, she said the added ingredients were herbs or ground up seeds that would help to speed his recovery. He suspected that they also made him sleepy at times, but he didn't try to stop her for he realized whatever she was doing was likely helping him. He noticed how Anna, her younger sister, seemed so devoted to her.

It was time for him to leave to try to find his own people. Unfortunately, he had nothing to go on. Talia did not know of the design of his emblem or the rays inscribed on his dirk. Tomorrow he would go for the first time to the great hall and talk to some of those there, perhaps even the lord of the manor, to learn if anyone knew of his people.

* * *

Talia woke up later than usual. She had not slept well. She knew Uberto was practically healed, except for his mind. Would he ever be able to recall his past? No matter, at the moment. She would have to tell him her plan and then ask him if he would help her. She regretted him having to learn of the shameful circumstances of her life. She had been readying herself and her sister, preparing for their departure. She heard Uberto moving in the next room and then he was up—looking at her from the doorway.

"Good morning," he said, stretching his arms toward the ceiling.

"To you also," she answered, still reflecting on what she needed to say.

"I'm feeling well today and think I will go to the hall to see what there might be to eat. Maybe I will find someone who can tell me where my people are located."

"There is nothing there to eat," she spoke quickly. "Sit down, Uberto. I have good bread and some honey to go with it. Besides, I have something I need to tell you." She turned from where she cut the bread to see him sit down on the other side of the table, a questioning look on his face. She hesitated before continuing. "I should have told you before, but now the matter is suddenly more urgent. I have been committed to marriage. In two weeks," she added.

"Then why did you. . ." loud knocking on the door interrupted his words.

"Yes, who is it?"asked Talia.

Without waiting for the door to be opened, a huge, wildly bearded man stepped in. His clothes were well made and fitted but soiled with dirt on one thigh. His demeanor was fierce and anger showed on his face. He look directly at Uberto. Turning to speak to Talia, he said, "So my charming sorceress, you have done it again. Taken in a wounded bird and set its broken wing. This one," he motioned to Uberto, "cleans up much too well. Send him on his way."

Talia turned away from the man to glance at Uberto, who remained sitting at the table. "It's true, my lord, he is mostly recovered from his injury, but the blow on his head destroyed his memory. He doesn't even know his people, or where they are located."

The man left Talia and lumbered toward Uberto, standing over him where he remained sitting at the table. "How convenient, no memory. You would like to stay here a long time and be cared for by my wife to be, wouldn't you?"

Knowing Wagnor's temper, Talia watched Uberto, afraid what he might say in response. She broke in, "He will be ready to leave soon, my lord."

Talia's words made no impression on Wagnor, who continued to stare down at Uberto. Uberto met Wagnor's gaze and answered in measured voice, "I appreciate what she has done, but now I am anxious to return to my people."

"Good," Wagnor answered, suddenly crashing his fist down on the table. "I want you gone by noon today at the latest. And don't try to take anything from here other

51

than what you came with or I will personally hunt you down and kill you." He turned away from him and went to Talia. Putting his hands on her hips he said, "You are much too kind, my dear. I will soon teach you to care for only those who are worthy of you." Pulling her to him, he gave her a mouthy kiss and then turned to leave saying as he went out, "Remember my words, man."

Uberto got up from the table and for a moment he and Talia looked at each other without speaking. Then Anna called out from the bedroom, "Is he gone, Talia?"

"Yes, he's gone," she answered, sinking into one of the table chairs, holding her lowered head with one hand.

Anna came to her and put an arm around her. In a soft voice she said, "I don't want you to marry him, Talia."

Talia lifted her head and faced her sister. Speaking barely above a whisper, she told her, "I don't want to, but I have no choice."

Uberto heard what they were saying and taking a chair next to Talia, quietly said to her, "You could come with me."

Talia turned toward him, her eyes locked on his. "He would kill you!" she breathed.

"I am not afraid to die. Since the gash on my head, I have no memory of any woman except you. You saved my life, and if I could save you from a marriage that could be worse than death, I would. I will help you if I can."

Talia reached out to grip Uberto's forearms tightly. "I would do anything to get away from that man. I have heard there is a nunnery far away in Brigantium. I would go there to escape him and I am sure they would take in my sister as well, especially as we have no mother or father. Would you be willing to risk taking both of us?"

"I have heard of the town but have never been there. If we did manage to escape from Wagnor it would be a hard journey for both of you. Riding hour after hour through the forests and meadows, spending cold and sometimes wet nights under makeshift shelters. It is not easy for a knight, let alone a woman and child. And if Wagnor should find us he will kill me, but what would he do to you?"

"He would not kill me. I am quite sure of that, though he would beat me. He wants my body too much to kill me. I would not let anyone hurt Anna," she said, pulling the girl to her and embracing her. She looked to Uberto, fear shining in her eyes. "Uberto, he would kill you! It is too much for you to try to save me from a wretched marriage. Walk away and he will leave you alone."

"I would rather take my chances. Knowing I may be able to save you and Anna is worth the attempt. I am not afraid to die. Besides, I have no memory of anything to live for."

Talia left Anna to embrace Uberto. "You should live, Uberto. You are young and strong. Someday, you will remember your past, and if not, you will have new memories."

Uberto returned her embrace, but withdrawing said to her. "We must hurry to make preparations before we leave. Certainly we cannot walk out together."

"Yes. Yes, you are right. I have an idea. Anna and I will leave shortly on horseback. She has her own mount but I will find a swifter horse we can ride. Then you can leave on Balustead, taking the western trail and we will meet up with you. With three good horses and perhaps divine intervention we should be able to put ourselves a great distance from the fortress before Wagnor finds out."

"Wait. One thing. I need a sword. A knight without a sword is scarcely a knight at all."

Talia disappeared into the adjoining room. Returning, she carried a sword in its scabbard and a belt. "Take this," she said. "It was my father's."

Chapter Six

Carina was glad when Leonardo gave her an excellent loom in a fine room overlooking the wide part of the courtyard. Though her working space was a bit smaller than the large room at her own manor, it did have a southern exposure and was well lit during the day after she opened the shutters. Her only misgiving was that it was not far across the hall from Patrizio's suite. The loom was not loud, the shuttle in her hands gliding smoothly through the threads. Sometimes Gina's toddler might cry, but he was generally little trouble for her and Gina was usually able to quickly bring a smile to his face.

Carina wasn't sure she wanted to work in a place so close to Patrizio. She was sure she would see him on occasion in the usual comings and goings of her day. Her thoughts remained for Uberto, whom she continued to keep in her prayers, as she was not totally convinced he was dead. Patrizio was a distraction. Somehow, he was able to make her forget about her husband—especially if she happened to look into his eyes.

As the days went on, Gina seemed happier, more able to forget her own tragedy, though on more than one occasion they were both lost in their own worlds of sad reverie, and once it happened that they looked at each other and embraced. The difference between nobility and peasantry were at these times minimal.

Gina kept asking her if she knew of any plans afoot to retake the manor and in truth Carina didn't know. At one point while visiting her sister-in-law, Antonia, she asked Leonardo about it, and he put a finger to his lips, hushing her from further questions. Apparently, something was going on, some plans were being made, but she was obviously not privy to it. There was nothing she could tell Gina.

Frequently, she happened to meet up with Patrizio by chance, opening the door to her workroom at the same time as he opened his door, and she would always lower her eyes. He would say nothing. That was how she wanted it. One day, as she was coming back from afternoon dinner in the great hall, she heard music coming from Patrizio's suite. She hadn't known he played, so she stopped in the hall to listen. The music came from an artfully strummed instrument and as she listened, she heard Patrizio's voice. It was a sad song, made even more melancholy by the tenor of his voice. She turned away to enter her workroom, but something in his voice stayed with her.

The sounds of the knights in training at times came to her if she listened, especially when the air was still. When she opened her shutters and leaned out her large window, she could see them in the distance on the field. Too far away to make out individual knights, still, she thought she could pick out Patrizio. The knights were spending more time than usual in practice, and someone had told her Patrizio didn't ordinarily train at all. She knew he was more interested in his books than training. Carina surmised the knights were getting ready to attack the Saracens. She feared for their safety.

She suddenly had some misgivings of how she had been acting with Patrizio. Never a smile, never a greeting, only a head bowed down whenever she saw him. She might never see him again if he was killed in battle trying to save her people. She should at least be civil to him. It wasn't his fault Uberto was gone.

Early one evening, while there was still plenty of daylight left, she had the stable boy saddle her horse and went for a ride. She rode beneath the walls of the town and then started toward the tiny harbor. Only two boats were there, one large and one small, and she rode past them along the beach toward the hills to the east of the town. The smell of the seaborne air was fresh in her lungs mingled now and then with a fishy odor. She rode her horse, Callista, at a leisurely pace, and long before she reached the hills she turned back.

Thoughtful, her eyes gazing on the flat, smooth stones that lined the shore, she didn't at first notice another rider coming toward her. Hearing the hoof beats, she looked up and saw Patrizio.

"We meet again, my lady," his dark eyes met hers.

Carina sighed. "No need to search for a piece of the one true cross."

"I'm sorry," he said softly as he pulled up to her.

Carina glanced at him, touched by the genuine concern she felt in his voice. "Someday, I suppose, I will get over him, though I will never forget him."

They rode in silence together toward the walls of the city. Carina thought about the music she had heard coming from his suite two days before. She asked him, "Did I hear you playing music the other day?"

"It is one of the things I enjoy, though I don't play often."

"I confess I listened a bit in the hallway and it sounded very nice."

"Thank you. I would play for you sometime though I would probably bore you."

"I don't know why you say that," she said, thinking that perhaps he needed encouragement.

"The few I have played for tell me my music is too melancholy for them."

Carina saw him watch for her reaction. "Lately, people would probably say the same thing about me." She spontaneously wanted to put her hand on his arm, but held back.

"I will play for you if you like."

Their eyes met and Carina smiled. "I would like that."

In the next few days Carina happened on Patrizio several times, but he didn't say anything more about his music. She sensed he was preoccupied with something, and she began to realize he usually did have something on his mind. She surmised they were ideas he found in his numerous books. She wondered if he thought about other things—like people.

Carina sensed a change in mood among many of those she met in Nice. She suspected it had to do with an expedition to her manor, but her brother, Renzo, would say nothing of it and when she approached Antonia, she dismissed her concern. Still, Carina sensed something was afoot. Thinking she might learn something from Patrizio, she boldly knocked on his door to remind him that she would like to hear his music.

Opening to her, he smiled, asking what she wanted. She reminded him, and he invited her in. She saw an open book on a large table and drawings he had made of stars in the heavens. "I want to show you something," he said, leading her to the table.

"You know of the wandering stars, I am sure," he began.

"Of course, the bright stars that somehow seem to follow their own course through the sky unlike all the other stars."

"What I have discovered, Carina, is two of the wandering stars have for several days shown a retrograde movement. In other words, instead of moving ahead of the other stars and the moon, they at times actually go backward."

"So?"

"Don't you see? The strange movement of these stars may actually tell us something about the nature of the universe. How we look at the earth and everything we see out there may be wrong."

Carina noticed he spoke with enthusiasm. "What do you mean?" she quietly asked.

"It may be that the earth is *not* the center of the universe."

"I respect your learning, Patrizio, but everyone knows the sun rises and sets each day as it goes around the earth. To think otherwise is unnatural."

Patrizio seemed completely unfazed by her objection. Taking on a teaching manner he said, "Sometimes what seems natural is not. Take a seat here and I will show you what I mean." She did as he said. Leaning over her, he pointed to circular lines made on the parchment. "See these drawings, Carina?"

Of course, she saw the drawings. How could she not? What she noticed more was the warmth of his body as he bent over her. She listened as he explained what the lines and points meant, but in reality, his elaborations held little meaning for her. Internally she reproached herself for her body's sensitivity to him, especially as scarcely two months had passed since Uberto was gone from her. She still hated to think him dead.

She rose from the chair, and catching him by surprise, bumped into him. Turning she faced him. "I'm sorry, Patrizio. I'm trying to follow your reasoning, but what you are saying is just not sinking in right now. Maybe another time."

"You wanted music, and here I am boring you with my observations and calculations. The sun will come up tomorrow regardless. I will play for you if you are still interested."

"I would like that, Patrizio," she said, immediately feeling more comfortable with the change of subject. While he went to get his lyre from inside a paneled closet, she stood up and walked about the large room, noticing the regal tapestries on the walls, the burnished weapons of war including two swords of different sizes, a shield and a crossbow. Then she noticed a sketched image of a woman's face done on sheepskin and mounted on a small, decorated wooden trencher. It was not a piece of art, but a simple representation of a person likely to have meaning only for a member of her family, or her lover. Carina wondered if Patrizio himself had made the drawing.

He was almost ready to play, and he gestured her to take the one comfortable chair near the window. She sat down, watching him as he readied his instrument. There was a knock on the door. Patrizio went immediately to answer it and she heard hastily spoken whispers behind the partially opened door. Closing it, he came back and set down the lyre. "We will have to do this another time, Carina. An important matter has come up."

Carina stood up, and gave him a quizzical look, which she was sure he saw but he said nothing.

He ushered her out quickly, and she felt something important was going on. In leaving she looked up to him saying, "Be safe, Patrizio."

Chapter Seven

Uberto casually walked away from the fortress gate knowing the worst was yet to come. Nevertheless, he was glad to feel completely recovered from the blow to his head and relatively secure with a sword hanging from his waist. He carried a few provisions in a sack. So far, the scheme he and Talia had concocted was working, and he counted on soon meeting up with her and her sister. The lack of long term memory remained disconcerting, but fortunately had no bearing on the present situation.

Once he had passed beyond observation from the gate he quickened his pace. He realized darkly, the success of their hazardous undertaking depended greatly on how soon Wagnor discovered his chosen wife-to-be was gone. That she detested him made no difference. As the son of a lord who had treacherously wrested control, he boldly presumed he could take any woman he wanted for his own. Uberto was prepared to fight him to the death if necessary, in hopes of liberating Talia from a life of misery. He saw her in the distance riding toward him.

"Glad we have made it this far, without being seen," she said.

"Now that we have joined up, we need to put many miles between us and Wagnor. Who knows how long it will take him to realize we're both gone." He held the animal steady while Talia dismounted to get on the other horse with Anna. "Are you ready for a fast ride, Anna?" He shaded his eyes from the sun with a hand to look at her. Then he quickly climbed on the horse Talia had been riding. Let's go," he said, starting at a fast pace along the trail with Talia and Anna following.

Uberto continued to lead swiftly along the rough road which gradually became narrower. He frequently looked back to make sure Talia and Anna were able to keep up. Difficult as he knew the pace must be for them, he didn't dare stop to rest lest they be overtaken. After hours of riding nonstop, even he had a sore bottom, and he rued his lack of conditioning. His concern was more for Talia and Anna and his regard for them grew as they kept up the pace without complaint.

As the daylight waned, Uberto began to look for a way to disguise their route. He spied a small stream running near the trail and entered it. He stopped a moment, to tell Talia to follow him on her horse while staying in the middle of the water so their hoof marks couldn't be seen. He led slowly through the stream for about a mile, and, as darkness began to fall, he looked for a place to rest for the night, confident Wagnor would not be able to track them.

Talia groaned as they dismounted. Anna said to Talia, "I can hardly walk," and rubbed her sore bottom through her tunic. Standing up straight with difficulty, they stiffly walked into the forest a short distance until they found a clearing of tall grass. Exhausted from the long ride, they tethered the horses behind two bushy trees and decided to make camp there for the night. It was too dark to go on, and Uberto hoped they had traveled far enough and fast enough to evade Wagnor.

"I have some food," whispered Talia, pulling open the drawstring of a pouch she had carried.

"What is it, sister?" said Anna. "I am so hungry."

"A slice of flat bread and a piece of pork. You can have a carrot too. You will eat too, won't you," she spoke to Uberto who stood near her.

"Thank you," he said, reaching to take a piece of pork from her hands.

They ate, and as darkness fell, Uberto looked for a place they could sleep. The ground was damp, but with his sword, he cut fronds and laid them near a tree trunk. Although she didn't complain, he knew Talia must be exhausted. It was important she get some rest as they needed to leave at earliest dawn to escape Wagnor. He had little doubt that he would be searching for them.

Anna may never have slept on the ground before, but as soon as she saw a place prepared for her, she immediately fell down on the rushes, curling herself into a ball with her head near her knees, and promptly fell asleep. Uberto saw the flash of Talia's smile as she looked at her.

"If we sleep together we will probably be warm enough," he said.

"I brought a thin blanket to spread over us," she replied.

Uberto noticed how her gaze lingered on him. They joined Anna—Talia on one side of her and Uberto on the other. He helped her spread the woolen cover over them. It was as coarsely woven, but hopefully warm.

Though Uberto still knew little about himself, he was learning more each day. It was clear he was accustomed to outdoor living. He was able to follow a trail by second nature to find his way through the forest, and his senses seemed sharpened by the open-air lifestyle. He soon fell asleep.

Dreams came. Confusing dreams, that he was unable to fully decipher. A woman who boldly glared at him, who at the same time seemed to call to him. A woman whose body he had tasted, who wrapped her arms and legs around him, clutching him tight. A picture came to him of her face seen by the light of a candle. A picture he tried to hold onto but one that seemed to keep fading away.

"Uberto, Uberto," he heard as he opened his eyes. In the dim light of morning, he found himself holding Talia. Inches apart, he looked into her eyes and she did the same. He felt Anna between them, her head at his hip, apparently still sleeping. Talia continued to look at him, and he wondered if she knew of his dream. Had he spoken in his sleep?

He shook his head trying to clear it, and she smiled at him. A warm, caring smile making him feel appreciated and admired. He turned away for a moment and then turned back to her, also with a smile on his face. He noticed for the first time, not her beauty, that he had long been aware of, but her spirit and warmth. She did not look away as he looked into her eyes, but instead continued to look at him, open he felt, to whatever he wanted to do.

Uberto knew her lips would be soft and welcoming, though she was not the woman in his dream. The woman whose face he could not quite recall. Awkwardly he moved away and then stood up, looking away and then back to her. He was attracted to her yet something held him back. "Dawn is breaking," he said.

"Yes, I know we need to leave soon," she answered quietly, not even looking at him.

"I was dreaming before waking this morning. Did you hear me say anything?" he asked. He gazed at her, wondering if she knew more about it than he did himself.

Talia was kneeling next to Anna, moving her hand gently over the girl's back. She looked up at him in a curious way. "I awoke to find you holding me. Was that part of your dream?"

Uberto found the question hard to answer. "There was more to it, to the dream, but I don't remember."

She turned from looking at him to the little girl. "Wake up, Anna," she said softly. "It's time for us to be leaving."

They shared breakfast standing, eating small pieces of heavy, unleavened dark bread washed down with water. Uberto saddled the horses and took them to the stream for a drink, and Talia gathered their few belongings. As he made his way back, he heard voices. Quickly tying the horses to a small tree, he moved forward, sword in hand.

He saw them through the rushes, three mounted men, all with drawn swords. Unmistakably, he saw Wagnor riding between the two others. The one nearest him was youthful and short in stature, garbed in a brown jerkin. The older man on the other side of Wagnor was portly and wearing heavy leather armor and a helmet embellished with gold filigree. Wagnor was the biggest of the three, his extra weight carried well by his large frame. Uberto stayed out of sight. Already, it was too late for him to alert Talia and Anna.

Now the three were out of his sight, though the direction they were traveling would soon take them to where they had bedded down for the night. Uberto remained hidden and stealthily approached their campsite. Through the shrubbery, he glimpsed Wagnor and the two others. He saw Wagnor addressing Talia from horseback, and though he couldn't make out his words, the anger in his speech showed in his movements. Because none of the men dismounted, he knew they were aware he was nearby.

Quickly, he considered his options. It would be foolhardy to rush in and try to vanquish all three of them. On the other hand, he could simply ride away and probably escape. He was sure their main goal was to get Talia back. They would prefer to kill him, but he didn't think they would go to great lengths to track him down if he ran away from them. To them, he was only a stranger. He conceived of a plan.

"Where is he?" Wagnor said again, louder and more threatening to his runaway bride-to-be.

"I don't know, I've told you. He just disappeared. Maybe he heard you coming."

"That would be like the coward he is," said the man in the jerkin.

"He may have gone to the stream to water the horses," spoke the older knight.

"No, he had already taken care of them," spoke Talia, her voice betraying a quiver.

"Are you sure, my lady?" spoke Wagnor, leaning toward her from his horse. "Then where could he have gone so suddenly?"

"I don't know, my lord." Secretly Talia was hoping the protracted questioning was giving Uberto time to get away.

Wagnor sat up straight and turning in his saddle surveyed the area. Talia sensed he was suddenly concerned. Leaving her and Anna, he joined the other two. She heard them speaking to each other in hushed voices. She bent down to hug Anna, whose fear was evident. She told her they would be all right, it was

68

Uberto they wanted. Even while she comforted Anna, she thought about Uberto. Her plan of escape from a bleak marriage now ended, she was hopeful that he at least would have a better life. .

Wagnor and the others left her, without saying anything more. Two of them directed their horses toward the stream, toward where she had last seen Uberto heading. The other took a more circuitous route. She resisted an impulse to scream to alert him, hoping that he most likely knew of their presence and by now had escaped.

They came back before long, and she breathed a sigh of relief knowing he had not been captured. Wagnor approached her. "So your wily scoundrel has flown the coop, taking both horses with him. Too cowardly to fight like a man."

Talia said nothing, but looked up steadily with hatred into his eyes.

"Good riddance, though he will die a quick death if he ever shows up again. Now, my lady, as you have no horse, you will ride with me and we will get to know each other a little better. I am not such a cad as you may think. In fact, I have many endearing qualities. Most of all, I recognize fine lines and spirit in both horses and women."

Talia again said nothing, though she thought silently, *you will never break my spirit, but someday I will shatter yours.* She had no respect for Wagnor or his kinsmen, who had usurped her family's legitimate authority by murder and treachery.

She mounted Wagnor's horse, sitting in front of him, and she steeled herself to his unwelcome nearness, particularly when he ran his hand across her back and then held the reins at her waist. She saw Anna, as she was helped up to sit with the older knight, leaving the man wearing the brown jerkin to ride alone. She braced herself for the long ride back.

The sun rose in the sky, a fine day for anyone who was not held captive. For part of the journey, the men had talked among themselves, though now only the uninterrupted cadence of hooves on soft ground could be heard. Her thoughts went to Uberto, seeing him as he reached for her in the morning. The heavy lidded tenderness she saw in his eyes, the yearning. Was it meant for someone else? The woman of his dreams? She wished she could be that woman. To be her was to know love— love that was pure and gentle and at the same time strong with desire. She sighed. She had never known such love and probably never would. And yet she had had a taste of love and would remember. It would help her to face what was coming.

At last they stopped. Wagnor insisted she get off first, though it would have been easier if he did. Was he afraid she would gallop off? She glared at him as she dismounted. He smiled in return, as if he liked to see her angry. She went to Anna who complained of a sore bottom. "I know, honey," she told her as if her words could make things better. The two of them began walking toward the woods when Wagnor's loud voice rang out. "One at a time, ladies. I don't want you getting any ideas about leaving." Talia looked back at him in annoyance. "As if we would run away in the middle of the forest," she tautly chided him. "You go first," she told Anna.

The short man carried the rations and supplies. He methodically began unpacking them from the well-stocked saddlebags.

"Hurry up, Josef," said Wagnor in an irritated voice. "We are not setting up for a picnic."

They soon finished their hasty meal and were back on the trail. All except Josef, who Wagnor impatiently left behind to finish repacking their provisions. They hadn't gone far when a loud, cut off scream made them stop and turn around. The men exchanged nervous glances and drew their swords. "We better check," said Wagnor.

They found Josef on the ground, unseeing eyes looking up to heaven and blood still pouring from a huge gash in his neck. "My God!" said the knight. "What heinous thieves!"

"Not thieves," muttered Wagnor. "The saddle bags haven't been touched. Uberto has been following us."

When Talia witnessed the sickening sight, her heart lifted. *He is not gone*, she thought. *He is going to save us.* She saw Anna bending down from her perch to stare at the man. "Look away, Anna! It will give you nightmares."

Talia quickly realized Wagnor wasn't nearly as concerned at the man's death as in preserving his own life. He and Gunther, she had learned his name, rode their horses in close circles near the dead man, anxiously peering out into the forest. Only after they concluded Uberto was not in the immediate vicinity did they make

Talia and Anna dismount before getting off themselves. They lifted the victim onto Josef's horse, tied him on it, and remounting hurriedly, galloped in the direction of their fortress.

Talia tried not to smile as she rode ahead of Wagnor on his horse. She knew, despite their numerical advantage, both men were afraid. Who would Uberto strike next and when? She didn't realize until now how far Wagnor would go to save his own life.

Chapter Eight

Carina didn't sleep well. In truth, she often didn't since the Uberto's presumed death. Getting up wasn't easy anymore. What did she have to look forward to? Today, however, she woke up with a worry. Had the knights left late in the night for her fortress? She dressed and immediately went to her brother's suite.

"Yes, they left last night," said Antonia who appeared disheveled and extremely worried. "I don't know what they were planning on doing. Renzo wouldn't tell me." She paced the room as she talked, head down. "A small scale operation apparently, leaving most of the knights behind to defend the city against attack if necessary."

"I'm sure they have well thought out plans; they had plenty of time. Still, the idea of them going with a small force is scary. Though Renzo knows the ins and outs of the fortress probably better than anyone."

"It's foolhardy, Carina, that's what it is." She leveled her gaze at Carina. "I knew they were planning something and I tried to talk him out of it. He wouldn't listen to me. Instead, he listens to his military advisors. He thinks he is doing the right thing, but he is so often wrong. Now he is staking his life on the success of their plans. He is too brave, Carina." She lowered her head and tears came to her eyes.

Carina went to embrace her. For a time, nothing was said. Then Carina spoke. "I worry for Amadeo as well, if they have not already killed him. They might take his life in retribution."

"Your brother has been in my prayers every day. With his bad leg. . ."

"I know. I pray for him too."

Carina went back to her work at the loom, unable to answer Gina's anxious questions. By this time, everyone knew that many of the knights had left for Renzo's fortress. No one knew for sure when they would return.

Toward evening, as darkness was falling, the small force returned. There was no joy in their demeanor. Seven knights had died and several more were injured. Already, Carina heard in the halls the cries and sobbing of mothers and wives who had lost their loved ones. She went immediately to Renzo and Antonia's suite and was glad when she saw her brother removing his hard leather armor. Antonia was with him.The two women went to each other and embraced.

"Any word of Amadeo?" Carina whispered.

"No, dear sister, we saw nothing of Amadeo," said Renzo. "We were unable to rescue any of our people. Only some of our horses."

Carina had much to think about. She worried about the people of her manor living under Muslim domination. She had already learned what that meant. Her people would be made to renounce God and to worship Allah instead. That is, unless they had gold. With gold or silver they could pay a yearly tax and be allowed to worship as they wished. The sad thing for Carina was that she could do nothing about it. Renzo and his aides would make battle decisions, and there was very little she could do to influence him. Besides, he would need the help of Count Leonardo's men to go up against the entrenched Saracens.

Somehow, the fight against the enemy reinforced the strong feelings she had for Uberto. She did not tell either Antonia or Renzo of her recurring dream. Was she crazy to hope he was still alive? Yet, if he were alive, why did he not come back to her? Had the Saracens taken him? Was she being foolhardy? She didn't care. Her greatest need was still to have hope.

The next day she found a new girl in her workshop—Myrna. Carina had been asking for help because without Gertrude, Gina couldn't supply enough yarn to keep her busy at the loom. She looked at the girl.

Of average height, thin, with a great stock of dark hair cascading in tight ringlets to beneath her shoulders. Carina knew to be careful when taking on a new assistant.

"Your mother has released you to work with me?' she asked.

"I have no mother, she is gone."

"I'm sorry," said Carina, immediately feeling compassion for her. "Your father can spare you?"

"Yes, my lady. I have two sisters."

"Good. There is much to learn and the way I will teach you may be different from what you already know." Carina turned and saw Gina intently listening to her every word. Gina was a reminder to her of how not to train someone, for Carina felt that Gina was at times a little too friendly and forward for a peasant. Yet, she had to admit, there were times when she appreciated Gina's open and generally cheerful manner.

Myrna nodded and seemed quite focused on what she was saying. Carina talked to her about simple things, like how to wash, card and comb the wool. She was satisfied the girl was listening and hopefully would not revert to ways she may have originally been taught. She looked more closely at her face; the child tended to keep her head down, and tried to imagine how she would grow into womanhood. Would she continue to be as meek as she seemed, or would she learn to speak up for herself?

"You can work for me," she told her and watched as the girl broke into a smile before quickly resuming her reticent manner.

"Thank you, my lady."

76

Toward evening Carina looked for Patrizio. She had seen him at dinner in the great hall, but only briefly. Something about his manner struck her as odd and she hoped he was all right. Missing him again at the evening meal, she went back toward her room. She glimpsed his figure in the corridor and hurried to catch up. On seeing him face to face, she immediately noted his dejected visage. Taking courage she asked him directly, "What is wrong, Patrizio?"

Without stopping, he turned to her, "Are you the only one who doesn't know of the failure of our mission?"

"I do. Yes, I do." She took long steps to keep up with his quick pace. As he said nothing else, she added. "I understand the mission was not a complete failure." He remained silent and she added, "I mean you learned of the enemy plans and brought back a great number of our horses."

Turning to face her, he angrily said, "I care little about horses. A woman died for me because of the beasts." He reached his door and opened it to go inside.

Carina sensed his emotion and said, "Tell me what happened, Patrizio." In her heart, she rebuked herself for being so forward.

"Come in, if you must know," he said resignedly, holding the door open for her.

Carina eyed the suite, noting how books and parchments littered the floor and the unmade bed, so different from her first time in his quarters.

"Sit," he said harshly, extending his arm toward a chair. He remained standing himself, and began pacing back and forth in front of her. "I was in charge of a few knights whose objective was to round up the horses in the corral and get them out through the gate. Everything went well at first. We had silently snuck up on the perimeter guards, our archers striking them down by the light of the moon. We were able to gain entrance into the fortress and most of the knights entered while I commandeered the corral and controlled the gate. At first, the surprise attack went well, but soon I heard the shouting of more and more of the enemy and the knights had to retreat against a swell of armed Saracens. They rushed through the gate and quickly mounted. My men followed immediately taking most of the enemy horses, escaping before they could mobilize. A woman screamed and I turned in time to parry a sword aimed at my heart. The man went down with my next thrust, but the woman's second scream was cut short and I saw her head roll from her body. I don't know who she was. She gave her life for me and there was nothing I could do but flee." He lowered his head and stopped pacing.

Carina saw how he stood there breathing deeply. She went to him and put her arms around him. He raised his head to look at her with curiosity. She backed away. "I'm sorry," she breathed.

He continued to look at her as if seeing her for the first time. Then he stepped to her and embraced her tightly, a long sigh escaping from his lips. "Thank you." Abruptly he released her and stepped away.

Carina was taken aback. She had felt much more than commiseration when he held her. Her body seemed to awaken in a manner she had not experienced since Uberto was gone. She regarded Patrizio and saw the beginnings of a smile. The air suddenly seemed charged between them. She wanted him to hold her again, but at the same time she didn't want him to for she felt it would violate Uberto. She didn't know what to say and looked away from his eyes, eyes that seemed to see through her.

"Are you still looking for a piece of the true cross," he asked, as casually as if he had asked if she enjoyed supper.

She had not thought about the subject for a long time. "Yes, I am," she stammered. "I want to find it," she managed to say in normal voice.

"There is an old Benedictine monastery mentioned in an ancient tome. From what I have been able to learn, the Benedictines share their wealth as well as their agricultural knowledge with their communities. This one is old enough to have shared in the greatest riches a monastery could own, a piece of the true cross. It is a two day ride from us."

Carina took a deep breath and looked at Patrizio. He remained an enigma to her. What possessed him to spend long hours searching through old records to find what she had hoped would solve her personal problem? Did he also hold out hope for Uberto's return? Why was he being so magnanimous? "Do you think Uberto is alive?" she breathed.

"We can only hope so," he said with a barely perceptible smile.

"Why are you so willing to help me?" Her eyes fixed on his.

Patrizio turned away from her sharp scrutiny. "I like you," he said simply. "I know all you have been through with the deaths of your father, my father and now Uberto is gone and presumed dead by most."

"Yes," she sighed. "Most people think so, and in truth, I myself sometimes find it hard to hold on." She lifted her head to look up at Patrizio. "I am very thankful for your kindness, Patrizio."

"When you are ready we will ride, taking of course two or three knights to ward off danger."

"I will be ready the day after tomorrow," she answered. A bright smile lit her face.

Chapter Nine

Despite Wagnor's urgency to return to the safety of the fortress, the foursome, and carrying the dead man, did not make for a speedy return journey. Talia's body ached from hard riding and she admired Anna whose face registered her discomfort yet she made no complaint. Darkness was beginning to fall, and they were still a long way from home. Wagnor communicated to Gunther the need to stop, and both men kept a lookout for a safe place. Talia knew their main concern was Uberto, the unseen presence they feared lurking somewhere behind them.

Wagnor pointed to a hill and they made their way up its gentle incline. Gunther and Wagnor removed the dead man's body from the horse and unpacked the food and blankets. Lacking other shelter, they would sleep on the ground. Talia rued the need to sleep with Wagnor and she prayed he would not try to take her in the night. She hoped Uberto was indeed following them.

Wagnor surprised her, for after they had laid out the blankets, he told her he would sleep next to Anna and Gunther would sleep with her. *Why?* She wondered, until in a low, menacing voice Wagnor said, "Anna is assurance you will not try to escape if Uberto returns. Do you fully understand my meaning? As much as we like Anna, a plucky young girl, she will not see the light of morning if you should be gone in the night."

Talia looked into his eyes and saw the self-satisfied smile on his face. How she would have liked to strike him there with all her strength. She turned away and looked out into the darkening gloom of the forest, hoping somehow for Uberto to save the two of them from Wagnor's evil clutches.

***

Uberto had indeed been following at a distance, alert for an ambush. With darkness falling, he was even more cautious. Knowing his enemy would need to stop for the night, his thoughts focused on how he might manage to rescue Talia and Anna. No doubt, Wagnor and his henchman would be ready for him. He was sure they would keep the females close. Bringing his horse to a walk, he studied the ground and saw where the party had veered from the trail. He noted the direction they had traveled.

Uberto instinctively knew the dangers of fighting in the dark. A misplaced blade could easily slash the face or sever the arm of a fellow combatant or hostage. He decided to wait until early dawn when he would be able to see. By then, Wagnor might think he had given up the pursuit. Moving further away from his quarry, he found water for the horses and let them graze before bedding down himself. He listened to the last plaintive bird calls before falling asleep.

At early dawn, he was up, moving stealthily, fully intent on what he intended to do. The spare horse he tied to a tree, and he carefully made his way back to where the small party had left the trail. Following their track, he came to where he could see a hill a short distance away. He stood undecided for a moment, then reluctantly tethered his horse to a sapling before moving ahead on foot. He hated to be without his horse for if either of the enemy had time to mount he would be at a severe disadvantage. He was relying entirely on surprise.

Continuing silently toward the hill, he heard a flutter of bird wings and he withdrew his sword from its scabbard. Crouching, he reached the rise of the hill where from behind a bush he surveyed the scene. Closest to him was Gunther. He was surprised to see Talia lying next to him. Several yards away slept Wagnor with Anna. Wagnor turned his head, uttering a sigh.

Uberto knew what he needed to do. Get Gunther first and then Wagnor. A surge of blood rushed through his veins and he sprung on Gunther, quickly driving his sword deep into his heart. Quickly, Uberto turned to strike

Wagnor, but the man was already up, sword in hand, wakened by Gunther's muffled scream. In front of him, his arm tightly gripped a terrified Anna.

"Let her go!" came Talia's loud cry from behind him, but Wagnor seemed to clutch the girl even tighter.

"Leave her and face me man to man," breathed Uberto in a low and ominous voice as he moved toward Wagnor with raised sword.

"Back off or she will die," he answered, moving the blade of his sword close to the girl's neck.

Uberto moved backward slightly, eying Wagnor murderously. Talia came to his side, facing Wagnor.

"If you kill her you will never have me," challenged Talia, her voice uncompromising despite her trembling hands.

"Give up the girl and you can ride away alone," said Uberto.

"How do I know I can trust you? You have already murdered two of my men."

"To free Talia and her sister from your clutches. I warn you, if you kill Anna you will die, but if you release her you will live."

Wagnor seemed to be thinking the situation through when Anna, struggling mightily, almost broke away from his grasp. He retightened his grip on her. "I know little of you, Uberto, but you are also a knight, sworn to uphold justice in the name of God and your lord. Pledge to me, by the Almighty God on high that you will not raise your sword against me, and I will set her free."

84

Uberto smiled. "You have made the right choice, Wagnor. You have it on my honor before God and man. If, . ." Uberto paused to make his subsequent words perfectly clear, "if you also promise to forever abandon your quest to make Talia your spouse." From the corner of his eye he saw Talia lifting her hands together.

"Then it is done," said Wagnor. "I will not pursue her." He released Anna and the girl ran to Talia and they embraced.

Uberto and Wagnor continued to face each other, swords now held at their sides. "Relieve me of my curiosity, Uberto. Do you plan to take her for yourself?"

"The Lady has her own plans of which I am not a part."

"Aha." Wagnor leaned on his sword, suddenly appearing more relaxed. "To a faraway nunnery then for the both of them. How noble of you to help her escape my lust. The God of the heavens must look very kindly on you."

Uberto had no answer for his biting sarcasm. He picked up Gunther's sword, unsheathed it, and gave it to Talia. Crossing to where the horses were tied, he quickly mounted one of them and told Wagnor, "Get on your horse and ride before I change my mind. You can return later to retrieve the bodies for burial."

"You should have killed him," Talia said as the three of them rode at a comfortable pace.

"I don't think he will come this way again," said Uberto with a nod of his head. "With two people dead already, who would want to ride with him? Besides, against a competent swordfighter how do you know I would win?

"I have little doubt you would, you are much trimmer and more athletic then him." Uberto noticed how she sized him up when she turned toward him. Continuing her line of thought she added, "You can't trust Wagnor. You know how grateful I am to you for getting us out of his grasp, but when you asked him to stop pursuing me, he would have said anything whether he meant it or not. He is not trustworthy, Uberto."

Uberto took heed of Talia's concern, knowing she knew Wagnor much better than he. They stopped for a short lunch, eating the bread and cheese they had procured from Wagnor's supplies. Not wanting to take too much time, they rode with speed along the trail, hoping it would meet up with the old Roman road. Toward nightfall, they still had not reached it.

Time to stop to find a place to bed down for the night, thought Uberto. He dismounted and led his horse into the woods followed by Anna, with her mount, and Talia who rode one of the horses taken from the men who were killed. She held the reins of the fourth, trotting beside her, which carried some of their few supplies. Uberto wanted to make sure they traveled far enough from the road so as not to be discovered by any robbers or brigands. The way was not easy going, by now they had all dismounted, and frequently they had to skirt around low lying branches so the horses could get through—not easy in the dim light. The scents of the woods assailed them, earthy, musty, and here and there, the heady smell of pine. Uberto became aware of another smell, unrecognizable and barely discernable and dismissed it as they came upon a tiny meadow and decided to stay there overnight. This time they had blankets, one to put under them and another to place on top. Anna immediately plopped down in the middle, the girl was obviously dead tired, and Uberto and Talia spread out the second blanket and bedded down on either side of her.

At daybreak, Uberto wakened to the faint sound of a female voice in the distance. He stood up, trying to hear it more clearly and saw Talia open her eyes from sleeping. "Do you hear that?"

She turned her head, trying to ascertain from where the sound came. "It's music. Someone is singing." She pointed. "I think it's coming from over there."

"Strange. I better take a look." Putting on his boots and picking up his sword, he made ready to investigate. He turned to Talia. "Arm yourself with the other sword, Talia, in case there is any trouble."

Uberto left her, keeping low as he moved toward the sound. Ascending a gentle rise, he saw through the trees a low-lying dwelling. On the other side of the knoll, he jumped across a small stream and stopped behind some bushes to get a better look. The house was of wattle and daub and in need of repair. It was situated in a clearing with a large garden on the left and a fenced in chicken pen and coop in the foreground. As he approached, the hens increased their cackling and a large white dog emerged from within the house. It stared at him, barked once in challenge, and remained near the entrance, on guard.

Uberto advanced, sword held down but ready, glad the dog did not attack. A woman came out of the building followed by three goats, two ewes and a buck. Then came three much smaller young goats—kids and another dog. Uberto smiled and raised his hand in greeting to the woman. She didn't acknowledge him, but stood with her hands on her hips watching him. He holstered his sword in its sheath and she motioned him to come forward

He stood before her regarding her closely and murmured "Grus Gott," thinking she was German. She appeared to be of medium age, somewhere between thirty and forty, with white skin and medium brown hair streaked with a little gray. Her tunic was dark red. She looked at him with curiosity.

"Why are you here?"

Uberto immediately knew that though she might be part German, she also spoke the old Roman tongue.

"We are traveling and stopped overnight away from the trail. We heard singing."

At his words, a smile lit up her face, subtracting years and revealing even teeth. "We?" she asked.

"A woman and her younger sister."

"I see. Then you are the only man?" Uberto noted she seemed wary.

"Unfortunately, though I would prefer to travel with two or three others for safety."

The woman looked away and with one hand patted the head of her dog at her side. She seemed to be in thought. She lifted her eyes to Uberto. "I would like to see the girl. If you bring her and the woman, I will give you good food to eat. Are you hungry?"

Uberto smiled. They had not eaten since noon of the preceding day and the very mention of food was already causing him to salivate. "Thank you. Thank you very much." He wanted to grasp her hands but didn't for fear of how the dog might react. "We have spent the night not far from here. I will get them."

"Really? A woman living by herself in the woods. Are you sure no one else was there?" asked Talia when he told her.

"No one, unless possibly there was someone inside the house."

"Funny she wants to see Anna." She reached for the girl and pulling her close, placed her hands on her shoulders."

"Maybe she just likes children," said Anna. "Let's go. I'm hungry."

Leading their horses, they walked through the woods to her dwelling. Tethering them at the edge of the clearing, they walked past the tame but curious goats who came up to them. The animals made walking difficult. "Get away!" said Anna to an ewe.

The woman came out of the house, and making pushing motions with her hands told the animals, "Scoot, you harebrained creatures. Shove off! Let them through."

She whacked one on its rump. "I'm sorry," she said, "they rarely see anyone but me."

The animals gave way, and the woman fastened her eyes on Anna, bending down to be closer to her level. "What a lovely girl," she said, almost with reverence. She got down on one knee and facing her asked, "What is your name, child?"

Anna glanced back at her sister before answering, "My name is Anna."

"How lovely. A beautiful name." She looked up at Talia and added, "You have a comely sister as well." Getting to her feet, she said to them, "I hope you have an appetite. Come, let's go inside."

The woman led the way, and Uberto needed to stoop to get under the short door lintel. She immediately opened a gate separating her living area from that of the animals, and they walked on rushes strewn on the floor toward a low lying table. The interior was dim at first until their eyes adjusted. It was illuminated by two small windows through which came bright sunshine, and dimly glowing embers of a fireplace. Clothes hung from wall pegs at one corner of the room, and at the other, a large, amber tinted quartz stone sat on a tiny shelf and seemed to glow.

"Sit, sit, sit," she said, pointing to cushions placed near the table. After removing a tight fitting lid, she dipped cups into the liquid and brought them to the table. "Enjoy."

They sat at the table savoring the sweet tasting mead and the full bodied porridge made of cut up chicken, carrots, onions, peas and turnips in a chowder of steaming goats milk. Hilde finally told them her name when she began talking about herself in response to their questions.

When they finished eating, she welcomed Anna into her arms, and leaning back, told how she and her sister fled the nunnery when a band of Saracens attacked it. Her voice grew ragged and tears came to her eyes when she described the horror of the massacre. She and her sister had hidden in the root cellar, and, when all was quiet, they escaped in the night, fleeing with the clothes on their back and the sacred wafers blessed by Father Rupert from the monastery. Hilde told how the hosts immediately brought them good fortune, for one of the sheep dogs followed them, herding three of the nunnery goats.

For days, they traveled on foot, drinking goats milk and eating roots, berries and any fruit they could find, knowing they needed to get far away from the territory seized by the Muslims. Finally, they settled on this spot, building first a lean too, then a shelter of reeds, and at last their present dwelling.

"Did God give you the chickens too?" asked Anna, turning around in Hilde's arms to look up at her.

"You could say so," she said, speaking softly to Anna. A man of God, a hermit who also lives in this forest came upon us one day and saw how we were doing. We talked for a time and I gave him one of the sacred wafers. He was so grateful he returned later in the year carrying a large bag holding two chickens and a rooster.

He stayed to help us make a place for them. He hasn't been back for almost a year. I hope he is all right."

Hilde was playing with Anna's hair, twirling it with her finger while she talked. She seemed content to have the girl in her arms. Anna seemed to like the attention. She asked her, "What happened to your sister, Hilde? Did she go somewhere else to live?"

Uberto had moved to be next to Talia. At Anna's question he saw Hilde sigh, and her face suddenly became troubled. Bowing her head she spoke even more softly as if to Anna alone.

"My sister took sick at the end of winter. I thought it was the grippe, for she had all the symptoms. She wouldn't eat and she could barely get out of bed. I tried to get her to drink a little, thinking her sickness would pass in time. But she got worse. I didn't know what to do, and there was no one I could ask to help. Just me and her. She became so hot, and I brought melted water from the snow to help cool her."

"Then she began to hallucinate. She began to imagine all kinds of terrible things—that the Saracens were at our door, that they were burning down our dwelling and assaulting us. I stayed close to Erwma and held her tight, but it was as if I wasn't there and she only saw visions. She became cold and then hot, breaking out into a sweat and then she became insensate. Her breathing became shallow and she seemed asleep. I thought that was good, that her body would rest.

"That was the beginning of the end. She only once became lucid, and then she seemed at peace. I gave her one of the remaining hosts; she took it calmly, smiled, and then went back into her sleeplike state. She never woke up after that." Hilde's eyes filled with tears as she finished her story, and looking down she wiped them away before glancing up at them. Talia went to her and embraced the older woman.

"I'm sorry, Hilde," she said.

"I will die here too," spoke Hilde soberly.

"No. You don't have to," said Talia. "Come with us. We have an extra horse and we are looking for the same thing that you want—a nunnery where we can live in peace and give glory to God."

"But my animals. Who will look after them? If I am not here to care for them they will not survive and will become prey for the wolves."

"Can you not leave them behind? Perhaps if we find a place and it is not too far we can come back for them," said Talia, trying to soothe the agitation in Hilde's voice.

Hilde lifted her head to look around at the inside of her home and toward the other side where the animals stayed at night. She placed one hand on Talia's. Looking at both Uberto and Talia she said, "I will stay here alone in the forest with my animals. I have my sacred hosts there in the quartz on my little altar. I am not afraid to die, even though alone."

"But, Hilde, if we find a place, would you not want to join the community where you would have friends and people who care for you?"

"I would like that. I would love to hear many voices lifted in praise. Would you do that? Would you come all the way back for me?"

"Hilde, if there is a way we will do it," answered Talia, looking toward Uberto.

Uberto only nodded in agreement. It crossed his mind the difficulty of traveling a long distance with a wagon in tow for the animals. He said nothing. He began thinking about the future. About leaving this place and about what they might find on the trail. How far had the Saracens penetrated into the interior of his country? Where was it safe to travel and where not?

With a fond farewell they left Hilde, each riding a horse with the fourth animal carrying their limited provisions and fresh goat cheese she had given them. They didn't know how long they would need to travel the little used trail before reaching the Roman road that would lead them to the region of Brigantium. There, they hoped to find the monastery and a nearby convent. Talia prayed it was not one of those destroyed by the Saracens—like the one Hilde had fled from. Hers had been closer to the Mediterranean, an easier target for Muslim pirates who controlled most of the Western Mediterranean and many of the towns nearby

They kept up a good pace, and when the sun came near the horizon, Uberto began to look for a place where they would spend the night. They came to a stream whose gentle waters they could have forded, but as the long shafts of the evening sun pierced the trees, a tall palisade appeared on a hill not more than a half mile away.

Thinking they would find shelter for the night, Uberto led them on, but as they approached the stockade, Uberto sensed something was wrong.

The place was quiet, too quiet, and the gate to the enclosure hung open at an unnatural angle. There were no buildings to be seen rising above the stockade and dark smoke poured from somewhere inside. No dogs or people greeted them. As they entered the gate, they saw why. The settlement had been completely destroyed.

"Let's get out of here," said Talia, an anxious look on her face as she turned her horse around.

"Wait," said Uberto. "The danger is past. The enemy that destroyed this place is long gone. There may be survivors. Certainly, it is a place where we can stay overnight. Let's go inside."

Somberly, they entered the broken gate, and followed the road. Once inside, looking to the right and left, they saw the remains of demolished buildings hugging the ground. Talia picked out what looked like a communal bakery, and they saw the shattered cross of what had been a small church or chapel. The corral for animals was empty, but grapevines hung undisturbed from their supports, their green fruit ripening in the sun. What appeared to have been the largest building remained partially standing. Asking Talia and her sister to wait, Uberto cautiously entered the wide front door hanging ajar by its only remaining hinge. There, cell by cell, he saw the humble sleeping quarters of a community of nuns, some with a garment or two still hanging from a wall peg. He crossed himself and continued, afraid of what he might find. Going as far as he could until the fallen roof blocked his passage, with a sigh he returned the way he had come.

"What is it Uberto?" asked Talia, sensing something was terribly wrong. She dismounted.

Uberto walked slowly the short distance to where Talia and Anna waited, Anna still mounted on her horse. With one hand on her shoulder, he somberly told Talia the bad news. "It was their home. All the sisters are gone. I don't know what happened to them."

"Is there no place safe from their terror, Uberto? These holy women, you know they would not even put up a fight. What have they done to them? God help us, Uberto."

Chapter Ten

The day was already brightening when Carina and Patrizio started toward the monastery. Three fully armed knights accompanied them, one of them, Guy, from her father's manor. He had been a friend of Uberto's, knowing him before she herself met him. They traveled at a good pace, for Patrizio estimated the trip would take one full day and most of another. Toward evening, he looked for a place to camp overnight, and they departed from the trail to find a place to set up their tents. A campfire was started, and they roasted fresh venison to go with cut bread and weak wine.

Carina sat with the men around the fire. She paid little attention to their talk about weaponry, of the phases of the moon and how they affect man's activities, and other discussions. At the moment, her head was lowered and her hands clasped the back of her neck beneath her flowing hair. She had a lot on her mind but found herself unable to focus. Uberto's death was too recent for her to be able to concentrate. This journey in search of part of the true cross, she had readily agreed to go on, but what did it mean without him? Why had she wanted to come?

She lifted her head, sensing movement, and saw that only Patrizio remained sitting, the others departing from the soft glow of the dying embers. "It's late, Carina, and we still have far to go tomorrow. You will share my tent with me." He got up and went toward it, leaving her sitting alone on the log.

She remained there a while longer, collecting her thoughts. She knew individual accommodations for women were not the norm when traveling. She trusted Patrizio, and besides they would both sleep fully clothed. Actually, it was not him she didn't trust, but herself. She followed him into the tent where she could make out his figure as he stood, head bent, near the apex.

"I will take this side and you take that side," he said. She noted his matter of fact manner.

She took a blanket from his hand, accidentally bumping into him, before becoming accustomed to the low light. Then, she dropped to her knees. Extending her palm as far as she could to the side, she saw there was more than enough room for two.

"Are you sleepy?" he asked.

"Tired, to be sure." She said no more and settled herself with blankets on her side of the tent being careful not to make bodily contact with Patrizio. She tried to sleep but soon realized too much was on her mind, Uberto in particular. She thought of their amorous times in bed together, and holding onto blankets pretended it was he.

Wiping a tear from her eye she straightened out and asked herself why she was acting this way, she hadn't done so in weeks. Uberto was gone and she might as well get used to it. She became aware, for the first time, of her own need for love. She was truly happy being married to Uberto and even her distress at her inability to conceive did not alter her sense of being loved. Carina did not fully reach the conclusion that night, but before she closed her eyes in sleep, she was not far from realizing she needed a man.

She wakened in the dim light of morning and found she had moved in the night. Her head was now close to Patrizio's. She watched him sleeping, the gentle inhale and exhale of his breathing, the composure of his relaxed features, the dark eyelashes, the growing stubble on his face and the surprisingly tender set of his lips. He was a man, a virile man, but he slept like a child. Carina had a momentary desire to waken him with a kiss. Instead, she tossed off her blanket and stood up.

He opened his eyes and looked up at her with a smile. "I dreamed of you."

Carina thought about what his dream might have been about, imagining many scenarios. "Yes?" she answered, her curiosity aroused.

"I should not have mentioned it. A man should not speak to a lady of his temptations."

"I see," she answered, looking away from him despite the sudden tremble she felt in her body. "You are right not to tell." Nevertheless, her mind continued drawing images, imagining the worst, or looking at it another way, imagining the best.

Carina continued to have mixed feelings as they continued on the trail. By now, they had reached the Roman road, and though it was in a state of disrepair, it was wider and more traveled. They saw merchants whose pack animals were loaded with cargo traveling in small caravans for protection against thieves, as well as wandering vagabonds and minstrels, monks, knights, and sometimes ladies, traveling in the protection of knights. They were dressed so differently—the colorful garb of the rich, to the grays and browns of the poor and those who sought not to bring attention to themselves. Nevertheless, the road was not well traveled as it probably was in Roman days, and seldom did they see more than one group at a time.

They moved at a more leisurely pace this day, and Carina spent time riding alongside Guy, who had been a friend of Uberto long before they joined the manor. She knew his wife had had a difficult pregnancy and delivery, but until the present moment, Carina had shown no interest in their child, a girl. Was it because she envied them their quick conception? Guy smiled broadly when asked about his daughter, telling Carina she was quite healthy, thank God, and had her mother's eyes. He continued talking about the girl and Carina smiled that a man should take such interest in a daughter, for there were many who would only profess such enthusiasm in describing the accomplishments of a son. At one point, she laughed aloud when he told her something truly unique about his one year old child. She resolved she would visit them and see the girl soon upon their return to Nice.

Toward mid afternoon, clouds began obscuring the sun and they saw fewer travelers. Those they did see seemed in a hurry. Upon reaching a bridge crossing a sizeable river, Patrizio confirmed they were close to the monastery. He asked of the next group of travelers if they knew how to find it. One of the men stopped reluctantly, and lifting his hood said, "Sir, the Saracens have been there. Hundreds of people have been slaughtered and anything of value has been taken. I wouldn't go on. It's not safe."

"Do you know where they are now?" asked Patrizio.

"They have commandeered the town. From there they send out raiders into the countryside. No one knows when or where they will strike next. We are in a hurry. If you must go, follow the trail to the right along the river. You will soon see it."

Patrizio turned to Carina and the others. "Do you wish to continue?"

"We are so close," she answered. "Besides, the horses might break a leg on the rough road if we tried to ride back through the night."

"The monks will give us shelter if the monastery has not been demolished," added Guy.

They took the road along the river and before long, as they climbed a hill, the stout fencing enclosing the monastery appeared. Ominously, they could also see dark smoke rising from a building. The smell of burning timbers suddenly engulfed them.

"My God, they have destroyed it!" said Carina.

They stood transfixed, staring at the destroyed buildings and still burning fires. There was no sound other than a wispy breeze making the tree leaves dance. Carina saw that Patrizio was keenly observing what remained of the monastery.

"The Saracens are gone and it is not likely they will come back soon," he said at length. "We can stay overnight in the building still standing."

Carina reined her horse. "I don't want to go in," she said to Patrizio and the others who were already leading toward the gate.

Patrizio turned in his saddle to face her. "Why not, Carina?"

"I have no desire to gaze at the bodies of slain monks."

"Stay with her, Guy, while we go inside and take a look."

Carina and Guy waited for what seemed like a long time. Finally, the others returned.

"There is a mystery here," said Patrizio. "We found no dead bodies, but many fresh graves have been dug just outside the wall. Each is marked with a cross."

"Strange," said Carina. "The Saracens would not have done it, but who?"

They eased their horses toward the unlocked gate, and on entering, Carina gazed at the destruction wrought on what had been a fair sized community. Most of the structures had been burned to the ground, though some were only partially destroyed. No livestock remained, though a few chickens scratched in the dirt near what was left of their coop. Without stopping, they made their way toward the only building that remained intact.

As they entered, Carina noted that the inside was relatively clean, strewn with rushes whose fresh scent did not entirely mask the odor of the men who had lived there. Going further in the hall, she saw the house consisted of a large number of small rooms, each with bedding on the floor and a roughhewn wooden cross high on the wall. Obviously, the monks' sleeping quarters. Without going further, she waited as Patrizio and the other knights checked all the rooms.

Patrizio returned holding a dirk in its holster. He showed it to Carina. "A fine weapon. See the engraving on the handle. Whoever left it behind will miss it. I give it to you."

Carina pushed his hand away. "I don't want a Saracen blade no matter how well it is decorated. My own dagger is good enough."

They froze at a loud knock at the door. The knights withdrew their swords from their scabbards and two of them went to the door. "Who is it," asked Guy.

"We monks," came the reply. The knights regarded each other with disbelief.

"Open the door," said one of the monks.

Carina and the others stood looking toward the entrance, wondering what they would see on the other side. "It's open," said Patrizio.

"Sire, most of our community has been barbarously murdered," spoke a resonant voice from beyond the door. Few of us remain. If you are Christians come out unarmed and we will welcome you."

"His voice is that of a countryman," said Patrizio. In a loud voice he asked, "How were you able to survive when the rest were killed?"

"We hid in one of the root cellars until they were gone," spoke a different man.

Patrizio pushed the door ajar and saw half dozen monks clad in brown tunics. He stepped out. "My brothers, by the Lord God Almighty it is good to see survivors."

Carina and the knights joined him and were swept up in the arms of monks grateful to see their countrymen rather than Saracens. One monk, however, held back. After the round of greeting and hugging ended, Patrizio asked, "Was it you who dug all the graves we saw?"

A husky, round headed man stepped toward Patrizio. "I am Father Einhard. With whom am I speaking?"

"Count Patrizio, of Nice."

"I am honored." He made a slight bow. "Yes, sire, we dug all the graves, perhaps not as deep as is the norm. Forty-one of our brothers lost their lives, including our abbot, our young priest, as well as four bedridden peasants in our care. Unfortunately, the tragedy does not end there. We also buried ten nuns slaughtered at the convent further up river," he pointed in its direction.

"Such good women. I hope to God none were held captive."

Patrizio bowed his head, as did Carina who also heard the conversation. "I am deeply sorry. The Saracen scourge is yet upon our land. We were able to beat them back at Nice at the loss of many men including my father and Carina's father. You may know their huge army was defeated at Tours by King Charles and Duke Odo. Still, they make inroads into our country and Charles cannot be everywhere. One day we will drive them into the sea."

"Yea, brother, were I a fighting man, I myself would gladly drive a sword through their breast. I can pray, and the Lord hears the prayers of His faithful."

"Not here, Father," said Patrizio, laying a hand on Einhard's shoulder. "To stay where the Muslims are in control is to invite disaster."

A young, short monk came forward and speaking with passion said, "We are not afraid to die. We will die to give glory to God."

Father Einhard immediately put his arms around him saying, "Brother Paul, when it is our time to die the Lord will take us home."

Carina noted the wild look in the man's eyes. She saw Patrizio also looking at him with concern.

In a calm voice Patrizio spoke. "Yes, you will die if you stay here. Return with us and you can rebuild in a safe place outside the walls of Nice. Wait," he said loudly, as Brother Paul attempted to interrupt. "Would it not be better for you to give glory to God your whole life than to have it cut off prematurely?"

Brother Paul lowered his head and turned to his right and then to his left. He shook with emotion and his hands balled into fists. "I am so angry. I want to receive the death of martyrdom as my brothers have already."

"Don't!" Carina stepped to the man and embraced his rigid body. "Don't believe God wants you dead. Patrizio has told you well. Come with us to Nice."

Carina backed away from Brother Paul. A strange smile suffused his face. "You are right, sister."

Nevertheless, Carina continued to have an uncomfortable feeling about the man.

The monks showed them their own rooms in the building, letting them choose any of the other cells they wanted. Carina was tired, and selecting one of the tiny quarters, tested the softness of the straw filled bed before lying down. She could hear Patrizio and Einhard still talking, no doubt making plans for the morrow. The tiny shuttered window above her gave meager light as dusk turned to night. From her sparsely filled bed she looked up at the barely visible crucifix on the wall. She prayed for all the monks and nuns who lost their lives, and she prayed for herself and for Uberto. As she drifted to sleep, she had the feeling her petition was heard.

****

Carina awakened to the delicious scent of roasting venison and soon learned the brothers had been up early making a hearty breakfast. They owed the main course to the hunting prowess of Brother Pedro, who before joining

106

the monastery had been an archer in the service of a duke. Since the former dining room was destroyed, they ate campfire style in a circle before glowing embers that radiated heat to help warm the morning chill.

Father Einhard and Patrizio were talking about the wandering stars. Carina listened, waiting to voice her question. She soon realized that both men tracked their movements, seeing in them the portent of things to come. She waited patiently as they discussed the question at length until she could wait no longer. Breaking in when Patrizio finished a sentence, she addressed Einhard.

"Excuse me, Father. Unaware of the Saracen assaults, Patrizio and I came to the monastery intent on learning if you may have been endowed with a piece of the true cross." She saw Einhard wince, as if in pain at the mention of the cross.

"Yes, my Lady, we were gifted with a piece of the wood enclosed in a silver crucifix. I am bitterly sorry to tell you it was taken along with the sacred chalices and vestments." He hesitated briefly, adding with invective, "They will rue taking the crucifix for whoever grasps it without fervor for the One crucified will suffer terrible afflictions."

Carina burned to ask one further question. "Father, Patrizio has told me the true wood of the cross has the power to bring healing to believers. Have you found. . ."

Einhard broke in, "There is no doubt. Many of our brothers have experienced firsthand the Lord's gracious curative touch. Not all, for we are mortal creatures whom God calls home at His appointed time."

Carina glanced at Patrizio, who sat on the other side of Einhard. He nodded affirmatively in her direction. Then he stood up saying, "Brothers, we are indebted to you for a delicious and filling breakfast, but we have a long way to go, especially since you will be walking. We had best get started."

Chapter Eleven

Talia wakened first in the early morning twilight. She had slept warm but not comfortably in the tight space afforded by her corner of the lean too Uberto had made for them. She had insisted to him that she did not want to stay inside what remained of the nunnery. Nevertheless, the horror the women must have experienced had wakened her in the night. She lifted her head. Anna and Uberto were still asleep, and in the tight space, she couldn't get up without wakening them.

Talia lay back, her thoughts going to her uncertain future. With the nunnery destroyed, what should she do now? She would be glad to stay with Uberto, whose calm leadership was worlds apart from Wagnor's manner. She would follow the man anywhere, but even though he could not remember, she knew he belonged to someone else. Maybe he would never find her. Maybe his dim memory of her would fade completely.

Uberto opened his eyes, remembering where he was. He turned and saw Talia awake, looking at him. He blinked, murmured something unintelligible and rose to his knees, careful to avoid hitting his head on the low, slanting wooden roof. Nodding to Talia, he extracted himself from the cramped enclosure, and went outside. She followed him, and he helped her stand up after she came through the low opening. They stood together surveying the desolation of burned buildings, broken fences, and overturned feeding troughs.

Uberto turned to Talia. In the morning glow, her face expressed not fear but a certain resilience. She turned toward him, her eyes meeting his until she lowered them. Spontaneously he reached for her hand, telling her, "We will find a place," though he did not know when or where. Closing her eyes, she leaned toward him and he kissed her gently and then held her. They stood together unmoving. A feeling he could not put into words came over him. He stepped back, uncertain. Then, speaking barely above a whisper, he said to Talia, "We need to prepare to leave. Before the Saracens return." He glanced at her and saw tears in her eyes.

"What is it, Talia?"

"The nuns," she said tersely. "What has happened to them?"

Despite the destruction, they found they could draw water from the well, and they also found carrots and cabbages to supplement what remained of the cheese Hilde had given them. Uberto wanted to proceed directly to the monastery. From Talia's earlier description, he knew it was close. If it had not been destroyed, they would meet with hospitality, and even if it was also destroyed, they might find some provisions not stolen. Furthermore, he hoped to get directions to a sizeable town.

He led them along the more traveled trail, hoping it would lead to the monastery. Riding a few paces ahead of the small party, he cautiously watched for any sign of Saracens. On reaching the crest of a small hill, he glimpsed through the trees a large stockade with surrounding farmland. Uberto immediately hoped it was the monastery, but as they got closer, they could see that most of the buildings had been burned to the ground.

Uberto and Talia moved ahead without words in the face of the destruction and probable deaths of the monks. Only Anna's voice broke the silence. "Looks like the Saracens have been here, too."

They continued on slowly, until Uberto held up his hand, whispering for them not to speak. He heard a voice and the whinny of a horse in the distance. They cautiously advanced, until standing on a rise, they were able to make out several horsemen, and six others who carried supplies and farm tools on their shoulders. Not knowing what to make of the scene, he told Talia and Anna to stay while he went forward to get a better look. As he came closer, the party spotted him and one of them lifted an arm in greeting. Uberto realized from their garb that the men walking were monks. Among those on horseback was a woman.

Returning to Talia and Anna to tell them there was nothing to fear, they urged their horses on and quickly joined the group. To his complete surprise, they knew him.

"Uberto, my brother, it is good to see you," a slender knight with dusky hair greeted him, embracing him while still on horseback.

"Uberto!" the woman cried, rushing to embrace him tightly with a fervor that surprised him, her eyes filling with tears.

He dismounted, as did the woman. She held him tight, her body pressed hard against his. Embarrassed, he tried to hold her back, looking into her beautiful eyes and noting how her full head of auburn hair gleamed in the sun. "Lady, I don't know you."

The woman seemed stunned by his words, and holding his hands she looked into his eyes. He faced her, this woman he did not know, and saw her hot tears. She shook her head no, denying his statement, and again leaned into him in embrace. "Uberto, don't you remember? I am your wife," she forlornly uttered.

Uberto again held her a little apart, scrutinizing her face, now registering sadness and confusion. Even in her present distressed state, the woman was beautiful, and he wished he could say he remembered if only to bring a smile to her face. But he couldn't remember, as much as he tried. Only something about the color of her lovely hair seemed somehow to have meaning for him. "I'm sorry," he finally managed to say. "I was struck on the head in a battle, a serious wound. Everything is gone for me other than recent events and the days of my childhood."

She looked at him, and he saw understanding come over her face. He also noted a determination in her eyes.

"Uberto," she said, "Even without your memory you remain my husband." She turned to Guy and Patrizio and the other knight who traveled with her. "Is not Uberto my one and only husband?" she asked. They murmured and nodded their agreement. She turned back to Uberto. "See, Uberto, everyone in the kingdom knows I am yours and you are mine."

Uberto stared at her. She was smiling now through the remnant of her tears and her eyes glowed with life and perhaps triumph. Though he could not remember her, she was claiming him before her own people. He smiled back at her. She was certainly a fine looking wife, and besides he admired her bravado. Taking her hand in his he kissed her, a light brush meant to tell her he was willing to try to be the man she married. She kissed him back with fervor until he broke away, eyeing her with interest. She boldly stared back, leaving Uberto with no doubt in his mind what she intimated. She wanted him.

Belatedly, Uberto introduced Talia and Anna and was in turn introduced to Patrizio, the knights and the monks. His old friend, Guy, tried to refresh his memory of how he, Uberto, and Wotano had ridden together before becoming knights and deciding to stay on at Carina's father's manor. Although unable to place Guy at all, Uberto listened carefully to what he had to say. Already he realized that his memory might never return, and if so, he might at least piece together his forgotten life from the memories of friends. He turned to notice Carina appraising Talia. Did his newfound wife wonder at his relationship with her?

Patrizio spoke the words to continue on. The now larger group proceeded along the road, the monks walking and the others on horseback, Uberto felt a sense of excitement. They were returning to the walled city of Nice. A city with memories he had forgotten, but a city that would hold the key to his future.

At the moment, Carina rode alone. She was deep in thought. Her joy at finding Uberto alive was muted because he did not know her. Nevertheless, she was thankful he was alive if not completely well. She felt lonely. All that she and Uberto had shared were her memories alone. They had experienced so much together. What would it be like to live with a man who didn't know the battles they had fought, their secret trysts, their blossoming love. She would tell him, of course, but to hear of their experiences would not be the same as living them.

Would he, could he, be the same man she loved? The memories they had forged, the understandings they had come to, even the differences they had bridged, they were all gone for him. Uberto would soon learn of her curse of barrenness, for it was common knowledge. He could not know of her scheme to restore her body to fruitfulness, for she had not told him. She wondered, would a piece of the true cross also cure Uberto's loss of memory? *Why not,* she told herself. If it could cure her, it could also cure him. She dropped back to talk with the monks.

"Brother monks, you are keeping up a good pace on foot today. Father Einhard, may I speak with you?"

"Of course, my child."

She dismounted, and holding onto Callista's reins, she walked alongside him. "Father Abbot, besides all the men who were slaughtered by the Saracens, I know you have also lost the sacred cross."

Einhard bowed his head and grimaced. "I would rather have died clutching it to my breast."

Carina felt his grief. She lifted her hand to his shoulder, saying, "I'm sorry."

He turned to her. "We carry on, my daughter. Life on this earth is a passing thing, beset with troubles but leading to eternal glory with the Lord."

Carina remained silent. Her thoughts were on righting things in the present.

"Father, do you think you will ever again be able to obtain a piece of the true cross?"

He turned to her and in a soft voice said, "It is my hope, child."

Carina's heart thrilled at the revelation. If he *could* get a bit of the cross and give her but a sliver, it would be enough. "How would you do it, Father?" She amazed herself at the boldness of her questioning.

"Only by going to Rome." He turned toward her.

Carina swallowed. Rome, the eternal city. A city set apart, surrounded on three sides by the hated Lombards. How could anyone go there?

"I know you are thinking it is dangerous to travel to Rome, Carina. For a simple priest on a mission to see the Holy Father, such travel may be possible."

Carina regarded him, awed by his courage. "You are a brave man, Father."

He turned to her smiling. "And you are a beautiful woman."

Carina looked away. His compliment was obviously sincere, but she did not expect it coming from a priest. She felt a bit unsettled and mounted her horse. As she left him to join the others, she looked back at him. A bit of a smile still lingered on his face.

She wanted to talk to Uberto who she could see was engaged in conversation with Guy. She wondered how she should approach him. She longed to hold him, for she had missed him terribly, refusing to believe he was dead. And yet, though not dead, all they had shared was gone from his memory. Even though they were married, she began to realize she might have to win his heart again. She felt equal to the task. Of immediate concern was his relationship with Talia.

To Uberto, it seemed as if everyone wanted to talk to him. He regretted having to say, "No, I don't remember" in response to Guy's questions. Guy had filled him in on many of the major things they had shared, but Guy somehow believed he would at least remember major battles or the deaths of Giancarlo and Carina's father. Uberto could sense the drama and the pathos of Guy's accounts, but only as a story, not as one who had lived through them.

He caught a glimpse of Carina riding forward to come alongside him. She didn't at first speak, just glanced in his direction. He studied her. Long, auburn hair flying in the wind, the rise of her breasts not quite hidden beneath her tunic, the slender waist and her eyes, green eyes that glowed with sincerity and a bit of mischievousness. Hard to believe, but from all accounts, she was his woman. From all appearances, he had chosen well. He smiled at her.

"Are you glad to be back with your people?" she asked, her free hand moving self-consciously to her hair.

"I am, though I find it still hard to believe. What good fortune to meet far away from our fortress outside a monastery."

"Not good fortune, but the answer to my prayers, Uberto."

"You must have missed me."

"You have no idea how much." She glanced at him and then lowered her eyes.

"I'm truly sorry I have no recollection," he offered. "I hope in time my memory will come back." He looked at her as they rode along together. She seemed to be letting go of a heartfelt sentiment.

"You were struck in battle and remember nothing of the conflict or anything that came before."

"Not exactly. I do remember my childhood."

"Your parents and your sister. You told me about your sister."

"I did? I will never forget what happened to her."

She reached over to put a hand on his arm. "I am sorry to bring up terrible memories."

"You know? I would not tell that to anyone." Uberto regarded her with disbelief.

"You told me she was killed."

"Did I tell you anything else?" He did not want to know and yet he felt he had to know what he had told her.

"Uberto, this is hard for me to say. You know what happened. Why do you want me to tell you?"

"Because if I told you what happened, including my part, I must have truly loved you." He saw her turn to face him directly, watching his eyes, her lips trembling.

"You hid from them and heard the screams of your sister when they raped her," she uttered, hating herself for doing so. "But, Uberto, remember, you were only ten years old. They would have killed you, too!"

Uberto again felt the stab of pain and sorrow he always did whenever he thought of that terrible day. Though still numbed by the memory, at his core he felt better knowing he had shared it with someone else, someone who did not reproach him for his cowardice. He indistinctly heard Carina's words.

"I'm sorry, Uberto."

Chapter Twelve

Carina was totally upset with herself. She had wanted to talk lightly with Uberto, to have him become at ease in her presence, to have him laugh and enjoy her company. She felt comfortable small talk would be a way to his heart. Instead, she had somehow stumbled into the subject of his deepest regret. She pounded her fists on the ground.

"What is it, Carina," queried Talia from the other side of the dark tent. "Is something the matter?"

"It's nothing," she answered, tightly closing her eyes in frustration. Not wanting conversation, she had gone to the tent before Talia and Anna.

"So fortunate for you to have found your knight," she continued.

Carina knew the woman wanted to make conversation. "Yes," she answered shortly.

"Too bad he remembers nothing since being struck in battle."

Carina sat up. She could see nothing in the darkness, but she heard Anna's steady breathing to her right and knew the girl was asleep. She decided if Talia wanted to talk, she had some questions of her own to ask. "How did you happen to find him, Talia?"

"Apparently he had been wandering in a semiconscious state and appeared near our fortress. I went in the evening to get fresh water from a stream and saw him. He seemed barely able to crawl. The blacksmith went with me the next morning and helped me to get him home where I could look after him."

Carina's respect for Talia increased markedly, but her misgivings remained. "I see. You nursed him back to health and then decided to leave with him."

"It's not what you're thinking, Carina. I was trying to escape an odious upcoming marriage and had learned of a faraway nunnery where Anna and I could safely devote our lives to God. Uberto agreed to take us there. In fact, only because of his swordsmanship were we able to escape capture. Now, with the Muslim destruction of the monastery and convent, I don't know what we will do."

Carina could hear in Talia's voice that she was upset. Again, she felt she had caused distress. "You and Anna will be safe in Nice," she vowed.

***

She awakened happy, knowing Uberto would be with her. Despite his lack of memory, he was there, alive and apparently well. She looked forward to his getting to know her better, as before. Her heart rushed as she thought of being in his arms again. She needed to take it slowly with him. His injury may have robbed him of the feelings they shared, the ardor born of their mutual love.

In time, in time, she told herself, he would feel what she did. Meanwhile, she would enjoy his presence. As if starting over, but this time there would be no doubt about the conclusion. He would love her as she loved him.

They ate breakfast and he sat around the fire with the other knights while she sat with Talia and Anna. She glanced at him from time to time, and she was glad to catch him also looking at her. When their eyes met, she looked down. Why, she didn't know. Maybe because he would read too much in her eyes. She felt she could barely control her heart.

On the trail again, she admired the monks, as they walked while the rest of the company rode. They were steadfast, keeping up at a good pace. She chatted with Talia, comfortable women's talk, and with Anna, who Carina could tell adored her big sister and would follow her anywhere. The girl's long, yellow-blond hair, blue eyes and light skin stood out handsomely against her kelly-green tunic.

She left them and rode ahead to catch up with Uberto, who had been talking with Patrizio. "Hello, my husband," she greeted him with a mischievous smile. She knew he was not used to the rediscovered appellation.

"Good morning, my lady. What, I wonder, brings your secret smile?"

"Thinking about all I know of you that no one else knows," she answered, still smiling.

"All my bad habits, I suppose."

"Of course, and much more." Carina noticed he seemed a bit on the defensive and quickly decided to change the subject. "Talia told me how you saved her and Anna from Wagnor and his men. I am proud of you."

He fixed his eyes on her, saying, "He is an arrogant brute and his family has usurped the lordship of the manor. I hope I did not make a mistake in letting him live."

"Your concern is for Talia and Anna?"

"Exactly. We are already a three days ride from their territory. Hopefully it is far enough."

They rode alongside, neither speaking for a time. Then Uberto said, "Tell me about me and you. How did we spend time together?"

"The usual things a man and wife do—eating, working, sleeping, listening to music and watching dancers, sometimes dancing ourselves. Sometimes, when I was sitting working on something, you would sneak up behind me and kiss me on the back of my neck." She smiled at the memory. "I loved it when it was just you and me and you played your lyre and sang to me."

"Now I remember," he said, putting his hand to his forehead. "My grandfather made it for me and taught me to play it. Was it a small one I played for you?"

"Quite small. I wondered at first how you could bring music from it."

"It must be the one. Do you still have it?"

"Yes. It's at the apartment Leonardo has given us. You would never be without it, even when traveling unless at war."

"I may still be able to play it."

"Of course you will be able to. You strummed it less than three months ago. Your fingers will remember." Uberto smiled broadly, making her glad. However, his demeanor quickly changed.

"I don't remember any of the songs," he said forlornly.

"Those you can easily learn." She didn't want him to feel sad.

"Wait, there is one," he said. "Only a child's song. I could sing it for you if you like."

"I would love it, Uberto."

"Trip by the river,
trip by the lane,
fox lookin' for chickens,
man lookin' for game.

Sun's on the meadow,
bright in the sky,
bluebirds are singing,
my, oh my.

Boy's gone fishing,
girl's making pie
supper's on the table,
my, oh my."

123

"Such a sweet song. I can imagine you as a child singing it."

Patrizio appeared from the front, riding hard. "Saracens ahead! Quickly! Get off the trail! We're going into the forest!"

"How many?" asked Uberto.

"At least six, maybe more, all fully armed."

They hurried the horses, monks and pack animals into the woods, trying to make as little noise as possible. Patrizio selected a defensible position, and the monks threw down their bundles and took up their saws, axes and scythes. Carina, Anna and Talia were told to stay to the rear, away from the line of combat. The knights drew their swords. Everyone stayed low to the ground, silent.

They waited for perhaps forty-five minutes and then Guy and Patrizio went together toward the trail. They returned having seen nothing of the Saracens. Quietly, the company moved again, this time the knights with drawn swords in the lead. The two women and the girl were stationed in the middle, followed by the monks who kept their farm implements at ready, prepared to drop their bundles at a moment's notice.

For miles, they traveled on high alert, ready to fight or flee, but no more Saracens were seen, and as the sun drifted lower in the sky they sought a place to spend the night. Not far now from Nice, they could have made it on the same day had everyone been on horseback.

Now that the danger of encountering the enemy seemed past, Carina rode her horse a little apart from the others. She was thinking of Uberto and how he would be with her when they returned. Would he share her room as she hoped? Or, on second thought, would he stay away from her, as he had no memory of their marriage or anything else about their life? She hoped he would stay with her, for she so wished for them to be together again, doing together the ordinary things of a married couple. She missed him, and now that she had found him, she resolved that nothing but death alone would take him away from her again.

As darkness was falling, Patrizio chose a place to stay overnight. This time the women prepared supper for everyone. Knowing they would be in Nice in the morning, Talia was apprehensive. She sat next to Carina as they ate, and asked about the city. Talia had never been in a sizeable town, and she wondered what to expect. Her eyes opened wide when Carina told her of all the shops. Talia learned more of Carina, of the manor she came from, and of her two brothers, one who was now lord of the estate. She realized they came from similar backgrounds, daughters of the lords of small manors. Unfortunately, Wagnor's family had deposed Talia's father. Nevertheless, Talia retained the bearing of a lady and not a peasant. In time, she and Carina might become friends.

In the tent, as they talked, Carina learned more of Talia's knowledge and experience with medicinal plants and curing salves. She came to realize the potions she had given Uberto may have had much to do with his return to health. Carina told her of Oriana, and suggested she might align herself with the healer. As for Anna, Carina had already offered her a kind of apprenticeship, where if she learned the intricacies of preparing and spinning different kinds of fibers, she would teach her how to use the loom.

Tired, Carina at last pulled the blanket over her. She was happy, for soon they would be safe again in Nice and she would have her husband back.

Chapter Thirteen

From a distance, Carina rejoiced on seeing the high walls of Nice nestled on the plateau. Home and safe, she thought. But, when the company approached the entrance the portcullis was not lifted. "Get close to each other," said a guard from above. They complied, bunching the horses and the monks together. Finally the heavy iron gate was raised.

Carina was not the only one who wanted to know the reason for the enhanced security. She would learn it from her brother rather than try to ask the guards. She looked around as they made their way to the stables. People were out and about as expected at midmorning, but she felt tension in the air. By the time she reached the stronghold, she knew why. War threatened.

Uberto went with Patrizio into the fortress. Uberto remembered it not at all. He was impressed with its massive construction. Patrizio and he went directly to Leonardo's suite, and barely knocking on the door, entered. Seated around a heavy table in earnest conversation were Leonardo, Renzo, Heribert, and Corrado. They looked up.

"Patrizio, you have found Uberto," said Leonardo as he and Renzo rose from their chairs to welcome them with open arms.

"Uberto, is something wrong?" asked Renzo.

Uberto recognized none of the men, and looked back to Patrizio, the only one he had come to know.

"Uberto was struck on the head and nearly killed," explained Patrizio. "The blow erased his memory. When our paths crossed he did not even know his own wife."

"I am sorry," murmured Leonardo, who didn't quite seem to know how to take the news. The other two men remained in their chairs but looked at Uberto with heightened interest. Leonardo faced Uberto, saying, "We have great respect for you, Uberto, for all you have done."

"My sister, Carina, somehow believed you were still alive," said Renzo. She will be so happy."

Uberto read the sincerity in their voices and eyes. "Thank you, sires."

"Sit down, my brother and Uberto," spoke Leonardo. "You have returned at a critical time. We are making plans for how we will face the enemy, either here or there. In your absence, we learned the Saracens have augmented the size of their army and our scouts have learned they are building siege machines. We believe they are using the people of Renzo's domain to construct them. We must attack before the siege engines are finished and before the Saracens have time to move them to Nice.

Uberto studied the battle drawings on the table and listened to the plans and to the ensuing discussion. He saw his place in the general scheme of the attack. He also learned the bishop would say a special mass for their success in the evening. His immediate concern, however, was the state of his own preparedness. Had he retained his skill with the sword? He had no memory of it, and though he had dispatched two of Talia's enemies, he had yet to go up against a skilled knight. He itched to test himself on the training ground, where even as they spoke, the knights practiced for the coming attack.

The meeting broke up in time for dinner. Uberto savored the aromas that came from the kitchen. He made his way to the main hall where a variety of courses awaited. Picking up a trencher, he helped himself, raising a hand to Guy who was just finishing. He briefly saw Carina who was leaving the hall and for a moment, their eyes locked until she turned and continued on her way out of the hall. His eyes followed the sway of her garment as she left. Hard to believe, this spirited young woman was indeed his wife.

Carina knew that Uberto had had to go to the war meeting. When she unexpectedly saw him as she was leaving the great hall, she hoped he would come back to their apartment after eating. She was disappointed.

Uberto sensed that she would wait for him, until he was ready. His immediate concern was the state of his readiness to fight in the upcoming battle. Finishing his meal quickly, he belted on his sword and made his way to the nearby training field. Well over a hundred knights practiced slicing at pells, the hanging contraptions with arms, or fought each other with wooden swords. On the other side of the field, pikemen drilled under the watchful eye of their instructor. Uberto walked toward those engaging in swordfights and waited. Two finished and one called out his name.

"Uberto, my God, you're back!" The man came quickly toward him, sweat still beading on his brow. "Uberto, it's good to see you," he said, hugging him tightly.

Uberto didn't know him, but was nevertheless warmed by the enthusiasm of his greeting. "My brother," he began,

"Uberto," rang out Guy's voice as he hurried to them. "An introduction is needed. Wotano, I want you to know about Uberto. In the battle at the manor, Uberto was struck in the head and has lost his memory. Uberto, this is Wotano. The three of us were fast friends, traveling the roads together, fighting for food and shelter, and singing along to your music before we saved Carina from the Giabaldies and stayed on to become knights of her father's domain."

Uberto took a good look at Wotano. Big and husky, but with the totally honest face of a youth. He could well imagine them being companions. Facing Wotano he said,"I'm sorry I do not remember, but I am looking forward to again getting to know you well, Wotano." He stepped forward to hug him. "There is always a chance too, of getting my memory back."

"We will ride together again, my brothers, on an expedition against the Saracens," said Guy.

"I need practice. I have no memory at all of whether I was good or not with the sword."

"You were excellent, and I am quite sure you still are," said Wotano.

"I think Wotano has himself shown marked improvement. You could clash swords with him for practice if he's willing," said Guy.

"Why don't you do it?" Wotano looked askance at Guy.

"He's bigger than me," Guy smiled.

"Not by much. You know size doesn't matter anyway in a swordfight." Wotano gave every appearance of not wanting to be the one to fight Uberto, but he nevertheless picked up his wooden sword and stood ready.

"The protective armor is there in the big box," Guy pointed out. "Next to it are the wasters."

Uberto walked over to the supply, selected from the hard leather armaments, taking time to fit them on correctly. He returned to face Wotano. He studied him, thinking how he might handle his sword. He didn't remember his own training, and hoped he had learned well enough for the attacks and parries to become ingrained. If not, he was in trouble.

"Start!" said Guy.

Uberto gave ground as Wotano advanced quickly, thrusting first and then slicing. Uberto caught his sword on his shield point and tried to push it down freeing him for a lunge to his midsection. The waster would not go down—the man was too strong. Uberto dodged a slice to his legs, and continuing to turn, quickly pressed his weapon toward Wotano's heart. He missed, but not by much. Wotano backed away, and Uberto realized he had the advantage of speed. Feeling a new confidence, he let Wotano take the lead. Parrying his thrusts while slowly giving ground, Uberto led him into a trap. He studied the rhythm of Wotano's moves until with one rapid movement, he caught his sword on his shield, pushed it to the side and lunged forward, landing a hard thrust to his heart. Wotano was pushed back but managed to stay on his feet.

"Bravo, well done." Uberto turned to see a small group of knights clapping to the side. Wotano stepped forward, sword lowered. "You always were better than me, Uberto."

Uberto looked again at the small audience. One of the men was extremely dark, and he had no memory of seeing anyone of such a color. Guy and the other two came up to him.

"Uberto, you probably don't remember Coco."

Uberto looked at the slender man, unable to recall. "He was in training with us. You knew him well. I have told him of your amnesia."

Coco reached forward to take Uberto's free hand in both of his. "You helped wife and me when we come to the manor with nothing. I never forget. You friend."

Uberto looked at him closely, trying to remember. A vague recollection came to him. Not the face, he didn't remember his face at all. "Would you say something to me again, Coco?"

Coco seemed puzzled. "What want me to say?" he asked.

"Now I know. Not clearly, but I do barely remember your funny way of speaking. We have talked before, haven't we?"

"We have much talked," said Coco, a smile breaking out on his face.

Uberto smiled broadly as well, and the two hugged. He wished he could recall more.

"Coco is the only one in training who came close to beating you," said Guy. "If you really want a test, you and he should battle."

Uberto regarded his newfound friend and his intention was to decline. He did not need to be told, there was always a chance of injury even using wooden swords. However, the beginnings of a smile played on Coco's face and as he watched him the smile grew broader as did his own. In his meek, foreign way, the man was giving him a challenge. A challenge Uberto would not turn down.

The others backed away and Uberto and Coco faced each other. Coco presented a small target—he was thin and wiry, and no doubt quick. His sword gripped at waist level, Coco advanced with his shield held high at arm's length. Suddenly he spun his waster around at a low level, aiming to cut off Uberto's legs. Uberto had not seen it coming, but he jumped away quickly, narrowly avoiding a painful blow, despite his leg armor. He eyed Coco warily, seeing what looked like a slight grin on his face. Slicing rapidly right and left, he backed Coco up, but his thrust at his chest landed harmlessly on his shield. He had not guessed how quickly the man could move.

Coco now took the offensive, lashing out with his sword at a speed Uberto could hardly imagine. Slicing right, left, thrusting, it was all Uberto could do to keep his shield between him and the dancing blade while he retreated. Yet he withstood the flurry, and thinking Coco had given his all, he instinctively prepared for a comeback. In the heat of combat, he didn't even feel the blow he had taken to his calf.

Imperceptibly to most, Coco's attack slowed as sweat appeared on his forehead. Uberto seized the moment to parry his slice, catching the butt of Coco's sword on the tang of his own. His weapon momentarily secured, Uberto lunged forward with his body pushing his shield hard onto Coco's. Coco tried desperately to keep his balance, but fell backwards, landing hard on the ground. Uberto rushed toward him, ready to finish him off, but Coco was not yet completely defenseless. Somehow, using his hands, he scooted forward in the dirt, striking at Uberto's legs with a quick whip of his foot. This time, Uberto was surprised. He fell to the ground, his shield clattering. Before he could rise, Coco was upon him, pulling back his sword arm to aim at his heart. Uberto rocked backward and brought his feet up toward Coco's hand and the oncoming blade. It flew from his grip. Despite the pain he must have felt, Coco landed on top of Uberto, ready to fight hand to hand.

Uberto caught the slim man in a bear hug and he began to laugh. "Coco, Coco, it's only practice. Let's get up and call it a draw." Coco stopped fighting and Uberto released his hold.

"Is leg alright?" asked Coco, still lying alongside Uberto.

"It hurts, now that you mention it."

"How about your hand?"

"Coco lifted his hand to take a look and moved his fingers. Blood oozed from his palm near his small finger. "Fingers all work. No broke bone."

Guy and Wotano moved to where they remained on the ground and gave each of them a hand to get up. "Great fight," said Wotano.

"A masterful performance," agreed Guy.

A bell rang, signaling the end of practice. Some of the men were going to the pond to bathe before returning to the stronghold. Uberto decided to go also, though among them was no one he recognized. On the way there, Uberto thought of his strange situation. People knew him, but he knew little of anyone other than Talia and Anna. Even his own wife, he hardly knew. Her love for him seemed real, but although he appreciated her beauty, his feeling for her was not yet deep. He hoped that would change in time. In the meantime, he needed to catch up with everything. He felt a strong need to learn more about himself.

Returning to the hall, he found more than enough to eat for the light evening meal. Guy was there in the hall eating with another knight, and he motioned for him to join them. Sitting down with them, Uberto learned that Arturo, the other knight, had recently lost both his wife and his baby. Not in any battle, but in childbirth. Uberto could feel the sorrow that still burdened the man. It reminded him of the death of his sister. The three men ate quietly for a time until Guy began talking about Paul. Uberto knew he was one of the monks who returned with them from the destroyed monastery.

"That monk is dangerous," said Guy. "Have you heard him rousing the people in the courtyard?"

"I know he's loud," said Arturo. "I try not to listen to what he is saying."

"Something about fighting the enemy. He's a monk. It makes no sense to me," said Uberto.

"That's it," said Guy. "He's urging the peasants to follow him in a holy war against the infidels. He says God will lead them to victory. All they need is faith."

"Faith without weapons and training will only get them killed," said Arturo.

"I remember him from when we and the monks came back from the monastery," said Uberto. "I heard some talk on the trail that he was upset because he didn't die like his brother monks."

"That's right," said Guy. "Patrizio had to restrain him from doing anything foolish. I don't know why he was acting that way. You think he would be happy the Muslims didn't find out where he was hidden."

The knights talked for a while longer on the subject and then Guy got up to go. As they finished eating, Uberto and Arturo also rose from the table. They left the hall together and were about to part when Uberto realized he didn't know the direction to his own place.

"I believe you are upstairs," said Arturo.

Uberto hesitated. "I'm not sure I want to go there," he confidentially said to Arturo.

Arturo stopped and turned to look at him. "Why? You've been away a long time. Your wife is probably there waiting for you."

"I know, but I know nothing of our life together. I have no recollection of our marriage or anything else."

"That is unfortunate."

"Very. It is rather daunting to go to live with someone who knows everything about you and you know almost nothing about her. To tell you the truth, Arturo, even the feeling I must have had for her is gone. To me, she is only a woman—an attractive woman, but nothing more. I find it hard to believe she is my wife."

"That is truly sad, Uberto. Even I, in all my sorrow at losing my wife and unborn baby, at least I can look back on some happy memories of our time together. But for you, life is beginning again. You will make new memories."

"Yes, I can start over again. And besides, some day I hope to regain what I have lost. How long it will take, I have no idea."

"If you wish, brother knight, you are welcome in my apartment until you are ready to return to the life you knew."

Chapter Fourteen

Talia liked working with Oriana. The old woman knew much about the healing arts that she was able to teach her. Talia herself knew some things that Oriana did not know. The two worked well together. Actually, at the present time, there was not a lot to do. With Angela also helping, the need for healing treatments was not great. They knew that with the likelihood of war imminent, that might quickly change.

Talia liked Angela. Oriana had told her of the girl's difficult childhood. By now, the girl was at least willing to talk. Not about any of the terrible things that she had experienced, but of the ordinary things women talk about, with the exception of talk about men. It was quite clear that she was still afraid of men. Even when they went to the hall for a meal, or shopping to purchase a few things for Oriana, Talia noticed how scared she became in the presence of the opposite sex. The girl would immediately drop her eyes and avoid any kind of contact with a male.

It was time to gather supplies. Oriana sent them out together to find wild herbs, roots, and other substances that were useful medicine. Talia was pleased to learn that Angela was no stranger to horses. However, because of the known presence of Saracens, they were to travel with two knights for protection. Talia had already conferred with those knights. She advised them that in no case were they to speak to or show any interest in the girl. Who knows what she might do if a man approached her?

She and Angela set out, walking across the large courtyard toward the stables. They heard much commotion across the way, and could hear a man speaking stridently to a crowd of people who were yelling their agreement to what he was saying. Angela looked to her, apparently wondering if she knew what was going on. "I think it's Paul, Angela, the monk I told you about. He came back with us from the destroyed monastery. He seems crazy to me. He was angry he didn't die with the others."

With Angela looking back frequently at the growing crowd, the two went on to the stables, got horses, and were joined by the two knights who were escorting them. Three hours later they returned, loaded with bags of medicinal plants, herbs, roots and aromatic substances such that the two knights accompanying them helped to carry it all. While they were away, however, the throng of those listening to Paul had grown even larger.

Talia could see how Angela's eyes grew wide and fearful as they made their way across the courtyard, still riding their horses, to the fortress. Thankfully, the knights helped them to carry it all inside and up to Oriana's apartment where she met them at the door, delighted at all they had procured. It took some time for the three of them to find a place for everything, but once they were finally done, Talia asked Oriana if she knew what was going on outside with the crowd.

"He is stirring everyone up. Telling the peasants they should march on Renzo's fortress. He says God is with them and the enemy will fall into their hands. A fool! Does he think the Muslims will lay down their arms when a mob of peasants descends on them with pitchforks and scythes? They need to be stopped before their blood is spilled at the walls of the manor."

"I thought the knights were going to do battle with them," said Talia.

"They are, they are, but no one knows when."

Talia could see that the talk of fighting was making Angela upset. The girl huddled in the corner of the room, head down and hand to her mouth as if she would vomit. Going over to her, Talia said. "We are safe here, Angela. Don't worry. Pray only that not too many of the men are hurt. If they are, we will do what we can for them."

A new voice, loud and commanding reached them. A knight, fully dressed in battle armor spoke from his horse to the crowd. Talia peered out the narrow window in Oriana's apartment overlooking the large courtyard. She heard the tenor his of voice but couldn't make out the

140

man's words. Whatever it was he was saying, the crowd began to disperse. Soon only Paul and a few others remained. The knight rode off, leaving behind a much smaller group. Talia wondered what he had said to them.

Carina, too, heard the commotion on the edge of town and was glad that Brother Paul had apparently been silenced, at least for today.

Happy as she was to have Uberto back, she as yet didn't share much with him due to his almost complete lack of memory. Moreover, though she was not privy to the deliberations of those in charge, she could tell that before long a large force would be sent to her father's fortress, now her brother's manor, to try to expel the Saracens. Such a task would not be easy, and she feared the bloodshed, especially of those she loved, especially her brothers and Uberto. Had she just got him back only to lose him?

With these fearful thoughts in mind, she went to visit her sister-in-law, Antonia.

"Dear sister, it has been so long since we have visited," said Antonia, coming to embrace her when she appeared at the door.

"Yes, I know. Ah, there's your little one. How she has grown already. May I hold her? And where is Lucio, the one with boundless energy?"

"He is with his tutor. Better there than here with Buttercup who may at anytime start crying."

"Oh, Buttercup," said Carina, holding the baby close to her face and cooing at her. "Are you really such a crybaby?"

"She's happy when she's sleeping and when she's nursing. Already she has the sweetest little smile."

"Can Aunt Carina see that little smile?" Carina asked, snuggling the baby even closer in her arms.

"Sit down, Carina. May I ask how it has been with you and Uberto?"

"Well, you know he doesn't remember anything of us at all. It is so difficult, because I want to start again sharing our life and he has no memory of it."

"I heard that, Carina. In time though, don't you think things will start coming back to him?"

"I hope so. I'm afraid. Afraid of losing him again. I know before long the knights will leave to attack our fortress."

"We are all afraid, Carina," said Antonia, reaching out to grasp Carina's hand.

* * *

While at table, Uberto learned there would be a special Mass that same evening. Knights were to purify themselves both in their hearts and in their bodies. He couldn't help but think this was going to be their sendoff to battle. He went to Carina's room—their room, to get soap and a towel. She was there, alone, seated, and slowly turning a spindle in her hand. She looked up at him, an inscrutable look he was not able to read. Uberto could not guess what was on her mind. He stopped before leaving to kiss her, surprised at the softness of her lips.

Leaving her, he hastened to join the others bathing in the stream. Afterwards, he put on the fresh tunic and outer garment Carina had given him. The bells of the cathedral rang out, announcing that the Mass would soon begin, a special Mass to pray for victory over the Saracens and ask God to protect the knights from harm.

Before the service started, Uberto returned to join Carina in their room. Immediately, on opening the door, he was taken aback by her beauty. Her hair hung long and shimmering down from her bejeweled tiara and she wore a soft white billowing gown cinched at the waist with a broad band of lustrous silk. The high collar of her glistening vest of royal blue, open at the front, gave her a noble appearance. Uberto dressed quickly, and when finished, again noted her beauty, instinctively lifting his hand to take hers. Together they regally walked the short distance from the citadel to the cathedral, joining the people of Nice streaming in.

Fortunately, space in front was saved for the knights and their ladies. Carina was glad to be in the company of friends, especially now as she felt so happy having Uberto at her side. Nearby were Guy and his wife and baby and Wotano with his family. Ahead, and in front, were her brother, Renzo, his wife, Antonia, and their two children.

Patrizio, and surprisingly, Talia and Anna also took the front seats along with Leonardo and his wife, Lucia, and their baby. Carina still missed her deceased father, as well as his sister, Dora, who remained at her manor. She especially missed her brother, Amadeo, who was now under the power of the Saracens. She continued to pray for him, hoping to soon see his cheerful countenance again.

The chanting of the choir ceased, and in silence Bishop Gregorio, four priests, and several altar boys processed from behind the ornate altar. All wore white vestments, symbolizing purity and victory. Carina held Uberto's arm after rising to greet the bishop. She felt comfortable and secure with him at her side. Nevertheless, she worried about the next day when he and the knights would attack the Saracens. She prayed for their safety. Finally, it was time for the sermon. Carina wondered what the bishop would say.

Bishop Gregorio walked slowly to the podium. Though an old man, he carried himself with dignity, his full head of white hair gleaming. His voice was still able to project through the church, and Carina listened as he spoke of the rapine of the infidels and the honorable goals of the expedition—to save her people from Muslim domination and to drive the infidels from the land. He spoke of purity of heart and likened the offensive to a crusade. Then he made a strong appeal for a fast from meat and from spousal intimacy until the knights returned successfully from the campaign. He implied so doing would make them strong and pure of heart, assuring victory.

Carina heard little more of what the bishop had to say. Although she looked straight ahead, she saw nothing. Engulfed with conflicting emotions, she at first did not know her own mind. However, the more she thought about what he said, the more she felt he was wrong. Especially for her and Uberto who had been separated for months. At last, she had the courage to squeeze Uberto's hand to get his attention. She looked into his eyes, searching for a sign that he also was not in agreement with the bishop's request. He turned to her, wondering why she had sought his attention. She realized the moment was long past for him. She would have to talk to him in the privacy of their room.

As the mass went on, Carina continued to stew about what the bishop had said. She realized giving up something for a worthwhile goal was laudable, but she could not see how not expressing love could be something the Almighty would desire. She certainly didn't think Uberto would be any weaker, for she had never known Uberto to express the least concern about doing anything arduous. In fact, he always seemed to enjoy physical challenges. The bishop was wrong; she had no doubt in her mind. Her only concern was Uberto. What did he think?

The hall was quiet that evening as Carina and Uberto went for a light repast. In observance of the bishop's request, there was no meat on the table. However, there was plenty of fish. People came in, ate quickly and left. Carina and Uberto did the same. Morning would come early and the knights would quickly be off to do battle. Tension filled the air. No one knew how many husbands, fathers and favored sons would be lost in the conflict. Everyone prayed for their safe return.

Uberto was quiet as he and Carina returned to their apartment. Carina still found it hard to comprehend his complete inability to remember everything in the years previous to his injury.

"You have no memory of our marriage, Uberto?"

"I am sorry, I do not."

"Yet you do believe we are married, don't you?"

"I do, and I have apparently made a good choice."

"Apparently?" She moved to stand close, face to face with him."

"Obviously, I should say." He placed his hands on her shoulders."

"I am sorry you have no memory, but I am yours, Uberto. I have been for well over a year."

"I believe you," he answered, his eyes fixed on hers. "We have lived as man and wife."

Carina impulsively embraced him, a sadness coming over her at Uberto's not remembering how they had loved each other. She lifted her head from his chest. "I love you, Uberto. I have loved you since long before our marriage. My only desire is to continue loving you."

Uberto felt her emotion and saw a tear in her eye. He wanted to love this woman; he wanted to make her happy. He wanted to build memories with her. He bent down to kiss her lips.

Carina closed her eyes and the memories of them together came flooding back to her. She held him tight, wouldn't let him go, and their kiss deepened.

Uberto tried to back away, and in so doing he stepped on her foot. "I'm sorry," he said, appearing flustered.

Carina was surprised and annoyed. She gazed open-eyed at him. "Don't you want me, my husband?"

"Did you not listen to what the bishop said? Of course I want you. I want you very much." He stared back at her.

"I want you too, Uberto. Please don't be angry with me."

Uberto stepped forward and took her in his arms. Carina felt herself quieted in his strong embrace. She felt the hardness of his body and the strength of his arms.

Already, the hour was growing late, and they prepared for bed. Carina took the inside and Uberto the outside. It was not a large bed, and it was quite likely their bodies would come together during the night. Carina knew sleep would be difficult for her. Nevertheless, she hoped Uberto would sleep well. He had to go off to war. Uberto blew out the single lit candle and lay down beside her. He gave her a chaste kiss.

Carina's mind was filled with images of other nights when they had been together. She tried to drive them away with prayer--prayer for Uberto's safety and success against the Saracens. Sleep eluded her. She listened to Uberto's deep regular breathing and knew he was asleep. She turned so her back was to his side. Finally, she also fell asleep.

Chapter Fifteen

Early in the morning before daybreak, Carina heard the tapping on the door. Uberto rose immediately and in a moment more was ready to go. She threw off the blankets and grabbed him, holding him tight and kissing him as if there were no tomorrow. "Be careful, Uberto."

"You know I will, for more than anything I want to come back to you." After one final kiss he was through the door.

Carina went back to bed. Her thoughts were troubled. When would she see him again? God forbid, would she see him again? Still lying in their bed, under the blanket she prayed for his safe return.

Later, she went to work, opening the door to the adjacent room where an assortment of spun wool and the loom awaited her. She opened the shutters to the two windows and saw the morning sun streaking across the courtyard where people already bustled from one place to another at the start of another day. Thankfully, on this morning she did not hear Brother Paul with his usual strident preaching.

Gina burst through the door singing, clutching her toddler, Oliver, with one hand and followed immediately by her seven-year-old daughter, who was already learning to spin.

"What brings such early morning cheer to you today, Gina?" asked Carina.

"The expedition, of course. Soon our knights will drive the Saracens from our manor and my husband and I will be reunited."

"I also hope we will win an easy victory. Unfortunately if there must be a siege, winning could take a long time and be hard on our people." Foremost on Carina's mind was her concern for Uberto, though she didn't mention him. Secondly, she thought of her brother, Amadeo, with his bad leg. She hoped he was all right.

"Anna should be coming any minute. I want to work with the loom today, Gina, so I'll have her work with you. You can keep her from making mistakes."

"She seems to learn quickly, milady. Ere long she will be as fast as Gertrude, I think."

Carina thought of Gertrude and smiled. "Ah, it will be good to have Gertrude back with us again."

***

For over four hours they had been on the trail, the army led by young Count Leonardo with scouts preceding him followed by almost two hundred pikemen and followed by Renzo, Carina's brother, now lord of the manor. Altogether over four hundred soldiers, including a dozen archers plus a few carpenters.. Patricio was not with them for he and a sizeable force remained at Nice to protect the town.

They stopped and rested, necessary for the foot soldiers carrying their long and heavy pikes. Soon they were on the road again, making good speed toward Renzo's domain. Four more hours and they would be at the outskirts.

Uberto rode comfortably with Renzo's knights, frequently sharing words with his old friends Wotano and Guy. Though not remembering their past together he listened carefully to everything said, learning sometimes from their offhand comments of what they had shared together in the past. Already he felt at home with them. Of course, much talk centered on their mission to wrest control of fortress and manor from the usurping Muslims. He remembered what the enemy looked like with their conical helmets and their coats of mail and he also heard all the talk about their skill with their long, flat swords and the proficiency of their archers with the bow. Like the others, he didn't know if they would come out to meet them or fight from behind the fortress walls.

As they reached a point where the trail widened, a muffled shout came from the front. Although no halt was called, the lines of men moving forward stopped and Uberto left the formation to join Renzo and his second in command, Corrado who moved toward the front. There they saw what remained of a massacre. Brother Paul and about a dozen of the peasants who had followed him lay on the ground in contorted positions, some with arrows sticking out of their bodies. Brother Paul's body was slumped in a fetal position, and underneath him he still clung to a large, five foot cross. Was he trying to convert the Muslims? Knowing the scouts were ahead making sure the enemy was not near, the knights took the time to check each of the men to see if any were still alive. Paul groaned when they turned him over and his eyes opened. He was the only one to show any life.

With a heightened sense of danger, the columns moved forward again. There was no time to bury the dead, at least not now, not knowing what they would face and how soon they would themselves be engaged in pitched battle. Soon, word came that the advance scouts had reached the woods at the outskirts of the manor. No one was to be seen. All was quiet.

Uberto took this to mean that the Muslims had been alerted to their presence. As the army approached closer to the manor, the absence of farmers tending their lands, of horsemen, of anyone was eerie. Even the birds were still. Were they walking into a trap? Leonardo directed the troops—a phalanx of pikemen filling the widened trail, with rows of mounted knights on each side of them in the trees spreading out a considerable distance. Cautiously, shields held in front, from three widely separate points scouts approached the walls of the manor.

Then, everyone heard it. The cry of an infant, loud and then muffled. But why was there no sight of even a head looking out over the parapet? Where were the mighty Saracens? Uberto wondered. Had the Muslims left after killing the able bodied men leaving only the women and children? Was this why there was no sign of a defense? As the scouts continued moving cautiously closer, Uberto did see a head, which from the distance, appeared to be that of a man. Surprisingly, he wore no helmet.

"Leonardo!" the man called out in a loud voice. "Renzo! Is it you?"

Renzo answered equally loud, "Is it you, my brother?

"Yes, yes, it is I."

"And are you safe? Where are the Saracens?"

"They are gone, leaving only old men, women and children, and me, a cripple."

The scouts continued to advance closer, now less fearful of being skewered by a volley of arrows. "Open the gate!"

Entering first, the advance scouts quickly verified that no Saracens were to be seen, only women and children and older men. Signaling the army, a company of Leonardo's knights entered first, followed by Leonardo himself, followed by some of Renzo's knights including Wotano and Uberto. Uberto looked around. Despite his memory loss, something did seem familiar about the place where he had first become a knight. He did not recognize the people, yet when Amadeo limped to greet him, some vague recollection came to him, something about riding a horse.

"My brother Uberto, so good to see you again," he said, embracing him. "How is my dear sister?"

Uberto had no idea who he meant, but Wotano accompanied him and quickly explained to Amadeo that Uberto had lost his memory after being struck by a Saracen sword. "I can tell you, Amadeo, that Carina is fine and very happy to have Uberto back after his long absence."

Suddenly Amadeo grew quite serious and earnest. "The bloody Saracens killed all the knights except me and this morning they murdered some defenseless men carrying a cross. Then they set off to meet ships on the Mediterranean. Their purpose is to attack Nice. Uberto, they have taken the young men of the manor to help in hauling siege machines and to put them together once they reach Nice."

"Then we are too late!" exclaimed Uberto, tightly grabbing the hilt of his sword. "How long will it take them, Amadeo, before they appear outside the walls?

"I think, I pray to God you have time to get back before them. Pulling and loading all the heavy equipment should slow them down. I want to go with you back to Nice."

Renzo and Leonardo also quickly learned of the Saracen intent and Leonardo, already mounted on his

153

destrier, cried out, "Knights, we must ride in haste back to Nice. The Saracens are on their way to attack our city!"

Uberto looked at Amadeo, wondering to himself if his faded memory was correct. "Amadeo, can you ride quickly?"

Amadeo looked with some puzzlement at Uberto and said, "You don't remember, brother? I can ride like the wind."

"You can take one of the horses carrying our provisions, said Wotano. I know at least one is now lightly loaded."

"Excellent," smiled Amadeo. I am looking forward to leaving this place and joining my sister."

Only a few other matters needed to be quickly settled. Those few men left at the manor would have to defend it as best they could. Fortunately, no known renegade bands or warlike strongholds were currently operating in the vicinity. It was determined the pikemen would follow the knights at a quick march, hopefully arriving at Nice before the Saracens. The leaders hated to leave them behind, for without the support of the knights they could be slaughtered. But a lightly defended town facing the full brunt of a Saracen attack was untenable. Quickly, the knights set off toward the walled city.

Chapter Sixteen

The shadows cast by the sun lengthened, and Carina was now left alone in her large workroom. It had been hard for her to stay focused, not knowing how the expedition and her husband fared. It was obvious that Gina, her best assistant was also nervous, though she remained bravely optimistic that her husband and all the people of the manor would soon be released from the captivity of the Saracens. Her youngest, Oliver, however, had been fussy throughout most of the workday except when he slept peacefully in his bassinet.

Carina thought about herself and Uberto. She was so glad to have him back but he was not the same. Physically, he was the same—fit, with slender waist and broad shoulders. Not exactly husky, but strong and supple. Yet, he didn't know her. She had thought he would have missed her, as she had missed him so much, but he did not. The sword to his head, she could still feel the ridge under his hair, had taken away from him all memory of their life together.

She needed desperately to talk to him. She had so much to tell him. Maybe then, he could begin to piece together in his mind their way with one another. Maybe, just maybe, he would again begin to understand the sweet and passionate way of their life together. But there had been no time. As soon as she had found him, he and all Nice was caught up in the urgencies and the preparations for war. Everyone knew that an attack was imminent. How could she talk to Uberto about her feelings at a time like this?

Closing up her workroom, Carina went to the great hall to eat. Some people were there, talking quietly in small groups, not nearly as many as when the knights and the pike men also populated the hall. So far, no word had come back of the expedition. Carina hoped that no news was good news.

Antonia came in, and seeing Carina she came to her table. "Carina, good to see you." She took a seat next to her.

"Yes, you too, Antonia. I'm surprised you are without either of your children."

Antonia sighed. "Thankfully, the baby is asleep and finally Lucio has settled down. He wears me out with his pretend battling with the wooden sword Renzo made for him. The hitting I am by now used to, but the yelling gets on my nerves. I'm nervous enough about what is happening at the fortress."

156

"I was always afraid when father went out to fight and now I worry for Uberto."

"That's all we can do is worry and pray. And bandage their wounds if they are not too serious."

Carina shook her head no. "I don't want to even think about that, Antonia. Tell me, is it true what I heard about the Saracens building siege engines?"

"All true. That's why we had to attack them before they have a chance to move them here. We drove them from the walls once, now they want to batter them down."

"My God, why won't they leave us alone?" uttered Carina.

The piercing horn at the gate sounded. "Maybe we have news," said Antonia, and both women quickly left the table and went outside the hall to where they could see the gate tower. They saw the drawbridge being lowered and the portcullis lifted. Then they saw the knights entering.

"So soon?" said Antonia, turning to Carina.

"I can hardly believe it," whispered Carina.

As the knights on their horses filed into the courtyard, Carina outpaced her sister-in-law in rushing down the stairs to the courtyard to find Uberto. Other women rapidly joined them in the yard eagerly searching for their husbands or sons. Hard to tell them apart, with each wearing armor and helmet unless a knight saw and called out a name. "Carina!" came a shout from her left. She turned toward the sound.

"My brother!" she shouted back to him, her heart suddenly filled with emotion. "My brother, you are back!" She rushed to be near him.

Amadeo guided his horse a little apart from all those heading for the stable and awkwardly dismounted. Before he could walk at all toward her, Carina was there and they embraced. "My sister, you don't know how wonderful it is to see you safe and free."

"Oh, my brother, I have longed to see you and to know you are no longer captured by the Muslims. But tell me, I have not seen him, is Uberto also with you?"

"Not to worry, sister. He is as hail and hearty as ever I have seen him. See, there he is toward the rear."

Carina looked to where Amadeo pointed, and seeing Uberto tall in the saddle, she spoke softly to her brother, "Amadeo, I will go to my husband, but I want so much to talk with you soon. So much has happened, my brother."

"We may not have much time, sister."

Carina had no idea what he meant, but turning, starting toward Uberto, she called out to him, and began walking toward where he still rode on his horse.

Uberto turned toward where he heard his name. "Carina, Ah, there you are." He dismounted and went to her.

They embraced, and Carina looked up into his eyes saying, "I am so happy you are safely back, my husband. Did you defeat them so quickly and easily?"

"No, Carina. They are coming here. That is why we came back so soon."

"You did not fight them?"

158

"They were already gone. They are coming by a different route, by sea, and transporting their siege machines."

"Oh, no! They are coming here again?"

"Yes, Carina," he said, standing close with one hand pressed against her back. "I don't remember the previous battle, but I have already heard enough about it. In our haste to get back to protect the town, we had to leave the pikemen behind. Hopefully they will make it back before the Saracens attack."

"You don't remember rescuing me along with my father and others?" She watched his eyes closely.

"I'm sorry. I still have no memory, though I have since been told what happened. Your father was a brave man."

"You were a brave man also, Uberto." A tear started down her cheek, and she turned her face away from him, hurt that he had no memory of what was so important to her.

"I am sad that I am disappointing to many people. It is a curse, Carina, to have no memory. One thing I know, I am trained to fight, and I am ready to fight this infidel nation that wants to conquer and impose their will on Christianity."

Carina saw the truth in his eyes and then pressed her body to his, arms holding him tight. "I am sorry, too, Uberto. You are a good man. When we fight to protect Nice, I will be there too, at the walls, doing whatever a woman can do to vanquish the enemy."

159

"Have faith in me, Carina. Give me time and one day I will once again be the man you knew."

Her eyes beginning to tear again, she told him, "You are, Uberto. You are."

Most of the horses had been returned to the stable, yet people still milled about. From near the fortress a horn sounded three times, the signal that an important announcement was forthcoming. Carina and Uberto walked together arm in arm toward the main courtyard. From the small balcony of the stronghold, Leonardo stood ready to speak and beside him were Bishop Gregorio, Renzo and Patrizio.

"My people, there is little time," spoke Leonardo. "We have just returned from Renzo's manor only to find that the Saracens have left. They are taking the sea route to Nice and may appear at anytime on our shore. This time they have built siege engines. We must immediately prepare for their attack. As you know, the knights have just returned. Our pikemen, not being mounted, are now hurrying back to join us to fight the Muslim attack. My people, we must be strong and brave and be ready to close any breaches in our walls. If the siege continues, we have enough food stockpiled to last for months. Our lives, our honor, and even our faith will be put to the test. Stand strong, my people, and we will drive the enemy to the sea."

Shouts rose from the crowd, cries of those anxious about their husbands or sons still on the way. Leonardo waved his hand to get them to stop. In a calm yet strong voice Patrizio spoke. "I know and feel your concern for the pikemen. It is our hope and prayer that they will soon join us in combating the Saracens. But we could not wait, and take a chance on leaving our city without most of her knights. That would be folly. We had to go on in all haste without them. Now, we all await their return. So far, we have seen nothing of the Saracens. When they come, we will be ready for them."

Patrizio's words were not entirely satisfactory to those whose loved ones were still on the trail. The volume level of the voices was reduced however, for now the crowd knew the reason for the knights returning without part of the army. One thing remained. Renzo raised his hand and in a loud voice spoke above the noise of the crowd. "Quiet! Quiet! Bishop Gregorio has something to say."

Elderly and white haired, the bishop nevertheless stood tall, still an imposing figure of a man. "My people, I have only one thing to say to you today. We stand, the people of God, ready to fight a foe who does not recognize Jesus Christ, our redeemer. Let us bend our heads and ask Jesus and Almighty God the Father to bless us as a people and to give strength to our hands and to our spirits. We fight in the name of the Father, the Son, and the Holy Ghost. Amen."

Turning slowly, he made the sign of the cross over the crowd.

"Now, we will prepare to fight," yelled Leonardo, his fist lifted high.

The crowd roared its approval, and even old men could be seen with their fists lifted high as the people dispersed noisily from the courtyard. Carina's arm was taken by Uberto as they began to leave, and she took one more look at the men still on the platform who had turned away from the audience and were now talking among themselves.

There was time to prepare, that was the good thing. Lookouts kept an eye out for activity along the shoreline. So far, no ships had been spotted.

Through the maze of people, Uberto and Carina made their way back to their apartment. Carina kept on the lookout for her brother, for she knew it unlikely, with the imminent attack, that he had been given a place to stay. "Amadeo! She called out on seeing him. He pushed his way through those going in a different direction and joined them.

"Where are you staying, Amadeo?

"I don't know yet. If we are attacked, likely somewhere on the ramparts."

"Stay with us, at least until another place is available. Uberto can get you armor and a sword."

"A weapon. I look forward to having one in my hands again. Especially to use it against the Saracens."

Carina looked more closely at her brother as the three of them continued to their apartment. She saw a change in him. He seemed no longer the calm and thoughtful scholar she knew; instead, his eyes disclosed a wild aspect she had not seen before. She felt she needed to talk to him, to talk when there was time, away from the immediacy of the impending attack.

"This way," she told him, as they entered the ground floor of the stronghold. Going up the stairs to the second floor, he entered with them.

Uberto left almost immediately, saying, "I will get you a sword and look for armor of your size, Amadeo."

After he left, Amadeo said, "I need time to think. So much has happened."

Carina turned to face her brother, her eyes showing the concern she felt for him. "What is it brother, that troubles you. What have you not told me?"

Amadeo took a step closer, meeting her gaze. "Sit down, Carina, and I will also. I will tell you how it has been with the Saracens."

She sat down on the edge of the bed and he on the one chair in the room.

"You know already, I think, about the knights. They rounded them up, took their weapons and killed them. Then they took their helmets and stuck them on sharpened posts around the fortress. That, the knights of Nice must have seen when they were ambushed months ago. Then, the Saracens erected a tower above the fortress where five times a day they made everyone bow toward Mecca, giving honor to their god, Allah. Anyone who didn't do it was beaten until they did. One of our archers, you may remember him, Leone, remained undiscovered and succeeded in putting an arrow through the man calling out the prayer in the tower."

Amadeo began to shake and he again dropped his eyes. Regaining his voice he said, "Sister, I will not tell you what they did to him, making all the people witness his torture. Finally, Leone died, and they made it very clear that such would be the fate of anyone who tries to oppose them."

Carina leaned forward from where she sat, her head down and almost touching the lowered head of her brother. She laid a hand on his knee. "I'm sorry, Amadeo.I am sorry for you and for our people. You have endured much. Nice is a strong walled city. The bloody Saracens will find it much harder to subdue us here. By God's will, when they come to conquer us, it is they who will be destroyed."

"I love you, my sister," he said, rising. Carina, too, stood up and they embraced. "I am going to the ramparts to see what I can do to help thwart their attack."

* * *

After getting equipment for Amadeo, Uberto returned to the rampart, and standing near the walls, he watched all the activity that swirled around him. Hot oil, lard and other caustic liquids boiled in huge vats near the walls, with buckets surrounding them for throwing their contents onto the heads of enemy attackers. Other cauldrons filled with water were being set in many places—to be used to put out fires. The main concern was the siege engines. Nice had less than two years ago withstood an attack of the Saracens, but that time the enemy didn't have a battering ram or catapults. That was what worried the leaders. Already carpenters had hacked down huge trees to be made into a massive bulwark to be fastened behind the gate. They waited only for the hoped for return of the pikemen to install it.

"Uberto!," a voice called him. Turning, he saw Amadeo approaching.

"Glad I found you. Ah, you have the armor and a sword."

Uberto lifted the sword in his hand and picked up the hard leather armor at his feet. "I hope we don't need these," he said handing them to Amadeo.

"I also," said Amadeo, who was already strapping on the gear. "The walls are strong, though who knows how much pounding they can take."

"We may have to make forays to slay those operating the siege engines. It will not be easy."

Somberly, Amadeo spoke, "They will be our own men, Uberto."

"What?!"

"They took the younger men of the manor with them. They had to drag the heavy siege engines and the Saracens will very likely have our people operating them against us. I know the Saracens. They will kill anyone who doesn't do what they want."

Vexed, Uberto momentarily closed his eyes and rubbed his fingers across his forehead. "We did not know this, Amadeo. Those accursed devils! Sacrificing our men, forcing them to operate the equipment without armor!"

"They would fight with us if they could."

"I will tell Leonardo and Renzo what you have told me, Amadeo."

Still seething with anger at what the Saracens were planning to do, Uberto left him. As he made his way along the parapet, he heard in the distance the sound of marching men, and as he turned to listen, the noise increased. He couldn't view the area outside the entrance gate from his position, but the commotion increased and he heard the lowering of the drawbridge and the lowering of the portcullis. Soon he heard cheering. The pikemen had returned.

Slowly, darkness fell over the town. Everything was now in readiness. Smoldering cauldrons, long poles with notches to push back enemy ladders, grappling hooks, archers each with chosen spots, and stocky tree trunks bound together blocking entrance at the gate. People milled in the courtyard and on the upper lane next to the chest high upper walls. Friends sought out friends, and men huddled together in small groups talking earnestly about what might happen next. Everyone knew the dangers—the chance of flaming arrows striking and igniting a building or of piercing a person. Attempts to scale the walls using long ladders, the battering ram, and by now, everyone had heard of the terrible catapults. Each person knew they faced death, but almost to a man and woman, they resolved to fight.

Time passed. Lookouts stationed in the towers saw nothing, and the consensus among those waiting and even among the knights was that they would not come until the next day. Carina had spent the evening with Antonia and her two children not far from the wall. With no sign of the enemy and the night wearing on, Antonia decided to put herself and the children to bed. Carina went with her back to the apartments and, yawning, decided she too would try to sleep. Not surprisingly, neither her brother nor Uberto were there. Would they get any sleep? She would be ready, if the horns sounded, to jump up and do what she could to fight the Saracens.

Talia also returned to her apartment, the one she shared with Oriana, Angela, and her sister, Anna. Fortunately, it was larger than most, for sometimes they needed to also bring in someone who needed their hourly attention. She was glad they had also secured the even larger space next door. It would give them some room to treat the injuries of civilians or knights hurt in the fighting.

Talia quietly slipped into bed, a bed she shared with her sister who was now sleeping. She thought pensively about her life, one that seemed always to be escaping someone. First it was Wagnor, who took her father's rightful domain and wanted her to be his wife. She was happy to have escaped that man's clutches. She would have been miserable living with such a proud and haughty man. Then, when she thought that she and Anna could escape to a nunnery, to be at peace and to give praise to God, that plan too was quashed by the Muslims. Now, the whole town was threatened by them. Was she ever to have any peace in her life?

Now, a new concern occupied her thoughts. New feelings, awakened first by Uberto, made her wonder if she had been right in fleeing to a nunnery. Wagnor was terrible, quashing in her any feminine thoughts she may have felt. Yet even since learning that Uberto was happily married to a good and lovely woman, her heart was still not at rest. She felt she knew almost nothing about men, but if one approached her. . .

She thought of Angela, poor Angela. Raped and beaten, living on the edge. Would she ever be normal? Would she ever be able to look a man in the eye? She felt sorry for the girl, and when she thought about it, her own concerns were nothing compared to hers. She wanted to help her, but didn't know how. Angela was a good girl, and she truly cared for the sick. If it was a man who needed attention, she was willing to help, but she held her eyes down lest he should look at her. Such fear! And yet she was young, recently turning fourteen.

Next, she thought of Brother Paul, the monk. The knights brought him back, more dead than alive. Already, the man showed signs of recovering, no doubt aided by the prayers of his brother monks. Mentally, as well as physically, the man was deeply ill. He muttered in his sleep of the deaths of the fourteen men who followed him to the manor. Lying on his sick bed, he would scarcely open an eye, his remorse was so deep. Talia agreed, he should not have done what he did. It was foolish to try to convert the Muslims. Their own religion, different as it was, she knew was somewhere around a hundred years old. A man with a cross and a dream was unlikely to change a conquering army. With all these thoughts running through her mind, Talia turned her head into the mattress, hoping to get some sleep before the Saracens attacked.

Chapter Seventeen

Carina rose sleepily from her bed. The bed she shared with Uberto. At sometime in the night she noted that he had come back to sleep. She was wakeful during the night, but noticed that Uberto slept soundly until he rose early in the half-light of dawn, quietly putting on his clothes, not even checking to see if she was awake. She made a sound. He turned toward her. She opened her arms to him and he came, bending to give her a kiss. "Be careful, Uberto," she whispered, embracing him.

"And you also, my wife." Turning he reached for something within the chest. He handed her the object, covered in leather "Take this knife that was given to me. Use it to protect yourself if all else fails." Kissing her briefly, he was quickly out the door.

She lay back in her bed, thinking about him. Uberto was back in her life but he was not the same. His memory was gone and with it much of his tenderness. Unless someone had told him, he would have no recollection of her falling into the hands of the Saracens when they attacked before, less than two years ago. He and her father and Giancarlo had come in the night to rescue her, and her father suffered a mortal wound. A tear came to her eye thinking about him. Now both men were dead. Only Uberto remained and he did not remember.

When she was captured, battling against those climbing the wall, why had they not killed her? Was the purpose of the Saracens to take her back to their distant harems? She could only guess that it was because of her too pale skin color, skin that burned rather than browned in the sun. So she had heard. A preference of the sultans for pale women. This time, if the enemy attempted to scale the walls, she would not be one of those pouring boiling oil on the attackers. She would find some other way to fight.

When she arose from bed, the day had long since broken and the loud chirping of birds gave no indication that this day would be different from any other. Carina felt restless. Everything was in readiness for the attack, save some last minute changes the knights would make as they prepared for battle. Certainly, today would not be a workday for her or her helpers. For now, there was nothing to do but wait until shouts and horns sounded the alarm that the enemy was sighted. She decided to visit her sister-in-law Antonia.

She knocked on her apartment door.

"Ah, my sister, I am glad you came." Antonia met her at the door and the two women embraced.

"Is the baby sleeping?"

"Yes, thankfully, in the back. No need to be quiet, though. With Lucio always so active, Buttercup has learned to sleep through everything. Have you eaten? I have some eggs, bread and fruit left over if you are at all hungry. I had no appetite this morning."

"I'll just have a piece of bread, thank you. I'm not hungry either. Uberto left early, before first light."

"Renzo too. He only said goodbye and left. I'm worried, Carina. This time, I know they have catapults."

"I know, I know. Uberto thinks our archers can pick off the men operating the machines. I hope to God he is right."

"Die! Die!" came a child's voice from the other room. He burst into the room bandying his wooden sword at an imaginary enemy. "Shh! Not so loud, Lucio, you'll wake the baby."

* * *

The early morning light brought a clear view out to the Mediterranean where quiet waves glimmered in the light of the sun. A fine, late spring day. Uberto was there early, almost alone at an outcropping of rock facing the Mediterranean. The south facing side of Nice lacked the high walls present elsewhere, for beneath it was a shear cliff dropping a hundred meters to rocks below. The most unlikely place for an enemy to attack, but one of the best observation points. As Uberto looked out to the sea, he saw no Saracens. His thoughts went to Carina, his newfound wife.

It was still hard for him to believe that she was his, for he had no memory at all of their time together. Not only that, though she was a beautiful woman, he found himself lacking emotion and feeling for her. And yet, he could sense her great feeling for him. They had been through a lot together, so she told him. She knew many things about him that he didn't know himself. She tried to tell him, perhaps in the hope of jogging his memory, but her efforts were useless. Often, one or another of those he talked to had already told him much of what she was telling him, but it was just not the same. To live through something was much more meaningful than to be told about something which one had no memory of.

Ultimately, Uberto felt he disappointed her, even when they had come together as man and wife. He wished he could be the man she loved, to feel the ardor she felt. He would try to be that man, but for now, he didn't know how. Most of what he knew about himself others had told him. One thing he learned on his own; he had not lost his skills. His riding, sword fighting and possibly military knowledge remained with him. He wondered at that. He had no memory of training, yet he knew from the practice battles with Wotano and Coco, that his use of the sword seemed ingrained. Maybe, he thought, once a skill is learned, it becomes so internalized that there is no need to think about it. Like walking, or riding a horse. Uberto shook his head again, vainly trying to shake out memories that just didn't come. He looked again at the shoreline. No Saracens. Maybe they were not going to attack.

"Ah, there you are," said Guy, who with Wotano appeared from the walkway. They too were wearing full battle armor. "Carina said at breakfast we might find you at the south wall."

"She did? I don't recall telling her."

"Anyway, still no sign of them?" asked Wotano.

"Nothing so far."

Later, when the sun was higher in the sky, they saw them, and even had they not, the blaring horns let everyone know. Those with sharp eyes saw the unloading of the heavy timbers of the assault machines from the ships. As morning turned to afternoon, everyone could see their massed cavalry and phalanxes of soldiers gradually drawing closer.

By evening, the city was surrounded. The tiny looking soldiers, due to their distance, with their conical helmets remained far from the walls. They stayed out of bowshot range. Nervously, the citizens of Nice and those in charge of the resistance watched the buildup of manpower on the plain. Those who watched from the towers and from the ramparts witnessed the size of the force facing them, a force numbering thousands. Yet so far, nothing could be seen showing that an attack was imminent.

The Saracens were keeping their distance. None of them could easily be felled by an arrow or even by a bolt from a crossbow. Behind the enemy tents that were being erected, those watching could see the war machines being put in position and assembled. Uberto, Guy and Wotano had at first watched everything from the virtually impregnable south of the walled town, but as the enemy moved to the north they also moved along the parapet to follow their activities. They passed many people standing on lookout or huddled around cauldrons of hot oil, boiling water and other toxic substances from the kitchen that were kept bubbling by hot ashes continuously sustained with added firewood. .

The day wore on, and the sun slipped under the horizon leaving a glowing red sky. It soon disappeared, leaving darkness illuminated by fires of the enemy below and the cauldrons above. So far, no attack, and all those milling around behind the strong walls of the fortified town wondered when it would come.

* * *

Angela looked at the kettle of boiling water. It was more than warm enough to use on her patient, Brother Paul, whose wounds needed bathing. Taking some in a bowl along with some centaury powder, which she mixed into the water, she went to attend to him.

Angela noticed how everyone was excited and she fully knew the reason. The Saracens had arrived. To an extent, she blamed herself, for trouble seemed to follow her wherever she went. Yet Oriana was teaching her the ways of medicine and Talia was always encouraging to her. They seemed to have more faith in her than she had in herself.

175

* * *

It was late, and Oriana had already gone to bed. A single candle provided the only light and Talia watched Angela as she again took warm water from where it had been heating at the fireplace. She saw her mix in some turmeric, a healing substance. She knew already what Angela was going to do—take it to Brother Paul to bathe his wounds once more. Angela looked up at her before leaving for the adjacent room. "Go and attend to him, Angela, and when you come back we must talk."

Soon, Angela returned, set the small kettle on the stand and head bent, stood in front of Talia. "Sit down, Angela. Sit down." Angela took a seat, but still held her head down, avoiding eye contact. "Angela, would you please look at me?" The girl raised her eyes in her direction.

"You know, of course, that at the present moment Nice is surrounded by Muslim soldiers?"

"I am sorry," she tersely answered.

By this time, Talia was used to trying to talk to Angela. She knew that somehow the girl tended to blame things on herself. "There is nothing for you to be sorry about, Angela. Their coming here has nothing at all to do with you. But, because they are here we need to be ready."

Angela raised her head to say, "I understand."

"There will be a battle and many people, both soldiers and civilians, will die. We must do what we can to help those who are injured. Angela, it is likely that even the larger apartment will be filled with the wounded. We may very well have to care for people in the hall. Do you understand?"

"Yes, I understand."

"You have already learned much, Angela, and I am glad you will be able to assist us. Listen to Oriana and to me. We will likely have to work fast, and despite our best efforts, many may die. Do not blame yourself for that. We gain nothing by mourning, only by caring for those who we may be able to save." Talia stood up and putting an arm around the slighter woman, ending by patting her on the shoulder. "Try to get some sleep, girl. We don't know how much rest we will have tonight."

* * *

Along the parapet, not far from the heavily buttressed gate, Uberto and Coco kept watch. They were part of the second guard, those who at this time would be the first alert in an attack. Besides those specifically assigned to guard duty, dozens of citizens manned the hot cauldrons and ladder poles to fight off an assault. Before leaving his apartment, Uberto was glad to have already won a minor battle with his intrepid wife, Carina, telling her she had no reason to be along the wall, exposing herself to a very possible onslaught of enemy arrows.

Now, except for softly spoken words, all was quiet. A three-quarter moon was rising in the east, beginning to show glimpses of the enemy troops and behind them their war tents. Uberto looked out at them, wondering what kind of people would send fighting men to the far side of the Mediterranean in a quest for the spoils of war. He had heard of their God, "Allah," but could not conceive of and certainly could not worship a God whose converts came by means of the sword. Placing his hand on the butt of his sword, he vowed to his God that he would fight this scourge to the end.

Suddenly, a hail of hundreds of flaming arrows rose from the ground, arching up and over the walls and dropping everywhere. Instinctively, Uberto and Coco raised their shields over their heads, but many civilians had no shields and were struck. Screams of the wounded came from many different directions and some of the houses began to blaze. The townspeople were ready with water to throw on the fires, but the arrows kept coming and those at the wells worked feverishly to keep them supplied.

Uberto was alert for what might come next— scaling the walls with long ladders. He turned around, seeing a flash of light. Coco was on fire! Fear filled Coco's eyes. A flaming arrow was stuck in the thick cowhide armor of his chest. Quickly, Uberto extinguished the blaze with a gloved hand, and then looked at Coco. Coco began smiling, and then pulled off his armor. The arrow lodged there had just penetrated through the thick hide. "Good I thin," said Coco, a grin on his face.

"Thank God!" said Uberto, giving the man a quick hug.

When finally the barrage of arrows ended, Carina hurriedly stepped out of her apartment and ran down the stairs to the outside. Fires were still burning to her right and left, but teams of people handled buckets of water to try to put out the blazes. Frantically, she rushed along the ramparts, dodging people and hearing the screams of those who had already found their loved ones—dead. She asked those she knew, "Have you seen him? Have you seen Uberto?" At last, someone pointed toward the high wall, telling her,

"He's over there!"

She rushed in that direction and found herself standing in front of him. Joyfully, she embraced him tightly. "Uberto, Uberto, thank God you are all right!"

Uberto returned her hug with gusto saying, "I am fine but Patrizio has taken an arrow."

Carina had not even noticed the man lying on the ground close to the parapet. Looking down at him, she uttered, "Patrizio!" She saw an arrow lodged in his buttocks.

"I am fortunate, compared to others, but the thing is painful and rather embarrassing sticking there," said Patrizio, in a quiet, strained voice.

"We must get him to Oriana," said Uberto. "She will know best how to remove the shaft."

"Yes, Yes," she answered. "I can help."

"Coco and I will carry him. He also was struck, but fortunately, the arrow did not penetrate far through his armor. Let's take him immediately to Oriana. You stay on the side where the arrow is so that no one bumps into it along the way."

The three of them made their way through the knights on guard and all the townspeople who were not engaged in putting out fires, who mingled, talking about the attack, ready for the next one.

The scene when they reached Oriana was pandemonium. Carina could see that the sick room adjoining Oriana's apartment was full of men and a few women lying on mattresses on the floor, some in agony and others who appeared to be sleeping, hopefully not dead. Talia moved among the injured, as did Angela and Oriana, applying bandages, healing salves, water and various liquid preparations. Brother Paul had apparently given up his sick bed, for he too appeared to be ministering to the wounded.

Talia turned when she saw them bringing in another injured, saying, "There's no more room for him here. He'll have to go in the hall." Then she took a second look. "Patrizio!" she said, shock registering on her face. Immediately she came to them. She saw the arrow still sticking from his buttocks. "Patrizio," she said, looking down at him. "Is that your only wound?"

"That I know of," he said gamely, wincing when she touched the arrow.

"Take him to my bed," she told them. "That arrow needs to come out right away." She led them to the apartment she shared with Oriana and Angela. "Here," she said, "put him down here. Careful, so the arrow doesn't bump against anything."

"Can I do anything to help?" asked Carina.

"No. I'm going to give him something to help with the pain before I remove it. It will take only a few minutes. On second thought, you could help cut away his tunics where he is pierced. Carina looked up at Uberto who also remained by the bedside.

"Stay and help if you want to" he said to her. "Coco, let's go back outside and see what is going on now."

The men left, and Talia handed Carina a pair of scissors and went to mix a concoction into some wine for Patrizio. He seemed asleep, but when Carina began cutting his garment he raised his head. "What are you doing, disrobing me, Carina?"

Talia came back, and answering him said, "We have to get the arrow out, Patrizio." She handed him a cup of wine with the herbs mixed into it. "Drink this. It will make the extraction easier for you."

Carina continued to cut away the cloth exposing his buttocks. She was more than a little embarrassed. Not so, Talia, who with a professional eye noted the site where the arrow entered. "Look," she said to Carina. "The angle it entered should allow us to remove it at his crack."

Carina looked to where she pointed, trying to keep the medical aspect of her words uppermost in her mind. "Do you mean you are not going to draw it out?"

"Not at first. The way these arrows are barbed, it would cause more damage than if I push it through.

181

Especially as we can cut off the point in the middle." She glanced at the cup she had given Patrizio. "You need to finish it all, Patrizio."

"That's not easy, laying here on my stomach."

"I'll get you a ladle. Do you feel anything yet?"

"I'm getting sleepy."

Talia left to get a spoon, and on returning, helped Patrizio get the remainder of the wine mixture down. She said to Carina, "We just have to wait a little more now. Are you all right with this, Carina? Not everyone is at ease around blood."

"I'm not sure. I would like to learn."

Carina stayed long enough with Talia to witness the arrow extraction. She even assisted in holding Patrizio while Talia steadily pushed the arrow through. The man sighed, breathing deeply, but did not cry out. When the barb was through, she watched Talia cut it off and then applying an ointment, pulled the arrow back out. Carina assisted until it was done and then sat down quickly, fearing she might faint.

"He was fortunate," said Talia, "had the angle been different, we would have to pull it out, and the barbs would cut further into his flesh."

"Yes," she answered weakly, knowing with certainty that she would never be one to pursue the medicinal arts. Regaining her composure, she stood up and asked, "How are the others?"

"Much worse, most of them. Some have lost much blood and we have had to tourniquet them. We need to find more clean cloth to stanch their wounds."

"I can do that. It is easier to make cloth than garments. We will make clean fabric and you can cut it into any size you need."

"Thank you. Thank you very much." She took a step toward Carina and hugged her. "It will save us the trouble of having to find old clothes, clean them and wait for them to dry."

Carina went back to her apartment. Uberto had finished his shift guarding at the rampart and was sound asleep in their bed.

Chapter Eighteen

Early the next day, the men charged with the defense of the city met in the parley room adjacent to Count Leonardo's apartment. Though not a particularly large room, it held a sizeable wood table with padded chairs on one side, with more seating on the other side. Seated at the table were Count Leonardo at center with Renzo at his left and Corrado at his right. Seated away from the table were Heribert, Uberto and Donato and Father Carlo. Conspicuous in his absence was Patrizio.

Count Leonardo, despite his position of leadership, was the youngest of those there, his youthful appearance particularly apparent in comparison to two of the old guard, Corrado and Heribert, both of whom had lived through many battles. Hard to believe that less than two years ago, before his father's untimely death, he was deliriously in love with the girl who was now his wife.

"Probably you know already that my brother took an arrow. Fortunately, it did not strike a vital area, and he

184

should recover in time. Men, we are faced with a conundrum. The enemy attack last night on Nice inflicted significant damage, but strangely, it was not an all out assault. There was no attempt to scale the walls, and they didn't use the two catapults. Why?"

"That will come," said Heribert. "Last night was only their opening volley."

"Precisely," interjected Corrado. "Today, after last night's barrage, they will want to talk, but only to demand our surrender."

"Surrender? We will never surrender," declared Donato, raising the fist of his sword hand.

"To be sure," averred Heribert. "Besides, what terms could these infidels offer?"

"I know what they would offer," said Father Carlo. "The same as at Toulouse. They will take our weapons and tax us heavily, taking anything of value year by year. Those who join their heathen religion are taxed less."

"And since we will not surrender, what then, Father?" asked Leonardo, pointedly.

"Death to all," he answered, bowing his head and quickly crossing himself.

"The women and children?" persisted Leonardo.

Father Carlo, spoke almost inaudibly, his head remaining lowered. "Death or worse, sire."

Uberto was moved but not surprised at what Father Carlo said. He had recently come from the strangely vacant nunnery and the massacre at the defenseless monastery. He did not know God's plan in all of this, but his own plan was sure. He would fight with all his

185

strength to protect the people of Nice. He would fight for Carina, for Talia, for his friends, Wotano and Guy, and for all the others and their families.

"I think we should try to fool them into thinking we are a small force," said Heribert.

"Why, Heribert? If they think that they may be emboldened into an all out attack."

"We will be ready. If they don't know at first that we have trained citizens prepared to turn back their siege attempts as well as trained pikemen, ready to set upon them when needed, we will retain the advantage of surprise."

"We have turned back the Saracens once already, though they had smaller numbers. What most concerns me is their catapults. That we have not seen before," said Renzo.

"Our walls are thick and strong. Giancarlo made sure of that. They will take a pounding. The archers will make it difficult for them to come too close with their machines," said Leonardo.

"Not only that, we will repair the walls if they begin to break. They are so thick, we can do it without too much danger to the repairers," spoke Heribert.

"Who should go, when they ask for terms of surrender?" asked Renzo.

"Not you," answered Leonardo. You have a growing family and we need your fighting skills."

"I will go," said Father Carlo.

"I will also go," said Heribert. "They will see the scars on my face, and know that I am a man used to battle."

Patrizio entered the room. He limped noticeably and his face seemed strained, as if he were in pain. He wore only his under tunic. "I will go to meet them," he said, quietly. "I have no one."

Everyone in the room looked at him, wondering how he could come so soon from his sick bed."

Patrizio, my brother, take time to heal, for this battle may be a long one. No one better than you may be able to conceive a plan to thwart the enemy."

"In that case, brother, I will go back to lay and rest. In truth, it is grievous to sit." Patrizio made his way slowly down the hall. He had correctly concluded that there would be a meeting to make plans, but he had not counted on his overwhelming weariness. The thought occurred to him that it might be a residual effect of the elixir Talia had prepared for him before she withdrew the arrow. Finally reaching her and Oriana's room, he suddenly felt faint, and opening the door, he looked forward to falling back on the bed. Seeing no one, he eased himself into the bed, laying on his stomach to avoid putting any pressure on his sore buttock. He wanted nothing more than to sleep.

Sometime later, he woke up, laying on his good side and feeling much healthier except for the continuing pain in his rear. A woman hovered over him, and blinking once or twice, he recognized Talia.

"Glad you are back in bed," she said. "You should not have left. I wonder, what was so important to you?"

"A meeting," he answered, dismissing her with a wave of his arm.

"We had no idea where you were. You are still weak and could have fallen down anywhere. Not to mention opening your wound."

Patrizio's anger was rising, but he felt too weak to fight her even verbally. "I did what I needed to do."

Talia sat down next to him on the edge of the bed. Her hand rested lightly on his back. She spoke in a softer voice. "I understand, Patrizio. It's just that your wound is in a bad place. Normal walking will aggravate it because you use those muscles. See," she gestured to the corner, "I've found you a cane."

"I am not an invalid or an old man. I will not be hobbling around on a cane!"

"Just for a few days, Patrizio, to give your butt muscle time to heal!"

Patrizio was exasperated. He knew Talia was trying to help, but it didn't mean he was going to do everything she told him. "You know," he told her, "I'm the one who is used to giving orders."

Moving her head even closer to his, she said with a hint of a smile, "Yes, sire. Do what you will, but you will be in pain much longer if you don't heed my advice."

"Leave me, woman!"

Quickly, she got up and went through the door. Patrizio couldn't help but think about her and about himself. He had never since childhood been in a position where he needed the help of others. He chose his own pursuits and followed them through. He knew little of this woman except that she was the daughter of a former lord whose dominion had somehow been stolen. She wanted to join a nunnery but it was evacuated when the Muslims came. Obviously, she knew much of medicine, and maybe he owed his life to her ministrations. Why was she so direct with him, not mincing her words as most people did with nobility? Why was he now still thinking of her? He had no idea.

She came back and stood over him. "You can go."

"You are throwing me out? Because I told you to leave?" The woman was beginning to intrigue him.

"Not that, Patrizio. If you are well enough to hobble through the halls, you can sleep in your own bed. I am willing to bring food to you if you leave your door unlocked."

"So you are not giving up on me entirely," he said, trying not to betray a smile.

"I would do for you what I would do for any man in your condition. But I would like to sleep in my own bed."

"Agreed. Hand me that cane and I will 'hobble' as you say back to my apartment."

"I will help you, Patrizio."

"No. I can do it. Just hand me the cane."

* * *

Outside, the peal of horns caught everyone's attention. From inside her workshop Carina heard it as did

189

her helpers, Gina and young Anna and Myrna. She quickly left the loom and hurried to find Uberto on guard at the east wall. She had seen little of him lately except when he was sleeping.

She embraced him, armor and all, and he held her. "What is it, Uberto? What is the meaning of their horns?"

"Most likely they want to discuss terms of surrender. Look, there in the distance. See them walking toward us underneath that canopy?"

Carina looked out over the parapet. "I see it now. Some kind of colorful fabric supported on four sides by men holding poles. But we would never surrender to them, right, Uberto?"

"Exactly, Carina. We have already discussed it and none of us is in favor of that. To do so would be to become their servants—giving up our arms and paying them heavy taxes. Instead of hearing the bells of the Cathedral, we would have to listen to the call to their heathen god Allah five times a day. I am told the Saracens have more numbers than when we fought them before, but we ourselves are more prepared. The difference is that they now have catapults."

"I have only just heard of them. Don't they throw things?"

"They do. Mostly rocks to try to break down the walls of the city. With their machines they can hurl almost anything, including animals and even people."

Momentarily covering her eyes with her hand she said, "I hate to think about it. Can't we do anything to stop them?"

Uberto sighed audibly. "It won't be easy, but I think we're going to have to try."

Carina grabbed him and holding tightly onto his waist, she looked into his eyes, "Not you, Uberto. Not you. Please! Promise me you won't leave the safety of these walls!" How well she remembered, it was her father who died on such a mission outside the walls.

Putting an arm around her shoulder and bending to her he said, "Carina, I will do what I have to do, but I also do not want to lose you. I will not volunteer for such an assignment, but if I am chosen, I will not turn them down. We all must fight against this enemy in any way that we can."

Carina pressed against him, afraid for him and for herself. She closed her eyes.

The sound of the horns again came to them, this time much closer. Uberto looked out. Now the canopy was drawing nearer. "We will have to go and talk to them. Father Carlo and Heribert are going. I'm not sure who else."

Carina and Uberto stood there with great numbers of townspeople peering over the walls looking at what was happening below. The edges of the colorful fabric fluttered in the breeze as it drew ever closer. Carina saw four men partially dressed in chain mail armor and another in the middle whose ornate garments bespoke royalty. Appearing from the left, four men from the city approached them. One stood out, Father Carlos because of his black garb and tonsure. The men marched solemnly toward the Saracens.

As the people of Nice watched from the walls, twenty-four archers took positions overlooking the proceedings. They would be ready in case of treachery.

Those representing the town and those of the Muslims now faced each other, scarcely two meters apart. The crowd along the parapet hushed as one of the Saracens began speaking, his speech punctuated by numerous gestures. When he was done, Heribert answered, his voice lower and barely audible. What he said could not be understood by anyone not down there, but his words had an obvious effect on his listeners.

Suddenly all except one of them became agitated, and in response, their main speaker raised his voice and extended his arm forcefully toward the walls of the town. Father Carlo spoke next, his shaven head bobbing as he apparently tried to ameliorate the situation, which seemed to be escalating between the rival groups. Whatever he said didn't appear to be working at all. Heribert turned toward the others to say something and then the group of four marched quickly and determinedly away, leaving the Muslims shaking their fists and shouting unintelligible words to their backs. It was apparent to everyone watching that the parley had not gone well.

"There will be a battle," spoke Uberto softly into Carina's ear as they watched from above.

"What everyone expected," she answered, turning to face him. "You do think we are strong enough to stop them?"

"I think so. They are a strong force, Carina. We will be tested."

"Hold me, Uberto. Hold me tight."

He turned to face her, noting her resolve. He bent to kiss her fully on the mouth before wrapping his arms tightly around her.

Carina melted into his arms. This was what she wanted, to be loved. To be loved by Uberto. Since he lost his memory, he had been different to her. He was civil and even friendly toward her, but it was not the same as before. Not the same as the feelings they shared together. So many times she had told herself, *He has lost his memory. How could he feel the same for me as before? It is too much to ask. Gradually, gradually, he will come to love me as before. I need to be patient.*

The hug ended, much too soon for Carina. She could see that Uberto's mind was already moving to things of war. Still, she needed to tell him, "That is how I remember you, Uberto. Holding me close."

"I will hold you close again, and often, my new found wife. But now, I must go to where Leonardo and his knights will learn exactly what happened down there."

Carina did not herself need to know more about the terms offered for surrender, as there would be none. She knew that Nice would be besieged, and that many lives would be lost. She could only hope and pray that the thick walls and military force would be strong enough to repel the attacks of the enemy. She went from the wall to go back to her workshop where she had left Gina and the two young girls at their work of making cloth for bandages. It was dull, repetitive work, not the quality she was used to in garments, but they were only bandages. With a battle looming that would decide the fate of the city and its people, time spent making clean dressings for the wounded was likely the best use of her loom.

Chapter Nineteen

Talia was faithful in caring for Patrizio. She brought him food three times a day and changed his dressings once a day. For his part, Patrizio seemed finally to understand the importance of allowing his wound time to heal. However, when she came to him this afternoon, bringing his meal, she found him in a very restless state. She found him with legs sprawled out on the floor leaning over an old manuscript. At least he was not sitting on the side where the arrow entered.

"Talia, look at this!" Setting his trencher of food down on the table, she knelt on the floor where she could lean over his body to look at the Roman script.

"See there," he said, pointing at the lines written on the paper.

"I see it, though the writing is faded and hard to read. Something about a machine that shoots large arrows at the enemy."

"That's it exactly. See, further down and on the next page it tells more about it. The Romans called it a ballista. Here, on the next page is a drawing. "

"So, an ancient Roman machine of war. Why are you interested, Patrizio?" she asked, turning from the manuscript to look into his eyes.

"Because, Talia, this kind of machine may be what we need to fight the Saracens. Quick, send for Giuseppe and his assistant, the best carpenter in Nice. And also, get Uberto. He will be the right person to operate it."

"Yes, my Lord," she answered, getting up from her knees. She exited the door, bent on doing his bidding, but wondering if the idea of building such a weapon from a few lines in a book was folly or could actually be done.

Uberto and the other knights were exiting from the large room Lorenzo now called "the siege room." He left quietly, though many of the others spoke loudly with bravado in response to the enemy demands. The news was not good. The Saracen terms required half of their gold and silver and other valuables. The Muslims would remain in Nice, taking charge of the citizenry and building a large place of worship using the toil of the populace. Those who wished to remain Christian would have to pay a heavy tax. If the town surrendered peacefully, the promise was that no one would be killed. Those who wished to leave rather than be subject to Muslim domination would have three days to travel to another site after which the Saracens would not guarantee their safety from attack.

The four men representing Nice did not hesitate to reject the terms of capitulation. Had the Muslims thought their force was so superior that the town would give up so easily without a fight? At that point, as told by Heribert, the infidels painted a much darker picture of what would happen if they encountered armed resistance. All those engaged in fighting would be killed, and their leader's lifeless bodies would be hung by the neck in the courtyard for all to see. What would happen to the women and children, they did not say, but their safety also would be in jeopardy, especially if siege became long and bloody. The warriors would exact their revenge.

Heribert expressed at the meeting that he could hardly contain his anger. If he had not known better, he would have then and there lashed out with his sword at the Muslim delegation. He and the other three who represented the town tramped away together, leaving the enemy still standing there, but before they got far, the man who was doing the talking yelled out to them in his broken dialect that they would have only one day to reconsider before the onslaught of the Saracens.

Before Uberto returned to tell Carina of the meeting, Talia encountered him and told him Patrizio wanted to see him as soon as possible. He went to his apartment, knocked on the door and was told to come in. He saw Patrizio on the floor, leaning over a large bound book.

"Come in, come in, Uberto. Glad Talia found you so quickly. Please excuse me for not getting up, but that arrow in my rear has caused me to assume some unusual but comfortable positions. You can help me."

"With what, my lord?"

"No need for formality with me, Uberto." He got up from the floor and with the book in his hands, gingerly took a seat on the divan. "The reason I sent for you... By the way, what kind of peace terms did the Saracens offer?"

Uberto proceeded to tell Patrizio about what they learned in Lorenzo's siege room.

"I thought as much. They think they will have an easy time defeating us."

"What do you think, Patrizio?" Uberto had learned that people held Patrizio's opinion in high regard.

"We are ready for them, much more so now than before. I don't think they will be able to launch a successful attack on our walls or gate. My concern is for their catapults. In fact, that is why I sent for you."

"Me? I know nothing about them."

There was a quick knock on the door and then Giuseppe and his assistant entered. "My Lord," he said, bowing slightly, and the other man did the same. Giuseppe was considerably huskier than his young assistant, and both wore shop aprons of tanned leather.

"Ah, glad you came when you did. This is Uberto. He will be important to our plans. Uberto, this is Giuseppe, the best carpenter in all Nice."

Uberto nodded to him, still having no idea what he was there for.

Patrizio opened the book in his hands. "Look at this, men." Moving over on the divan, he added, "Giuseppe, sit here with me, and Uberto and your assistant can stand close. On this page is a drawing of a Roman ballista. Take a good look at it."

Uberto bent down at the side of the divan to take a good look at the machine. He had never seen anything like it.

"So, this is a weapon of war," commented Giuseppe, bending closer to get a better look at it. "Too bad the drawing is not clearer."

"The arms make it look something like a huge bow," said Uberto.

"Exactly," concurred Patrizio. "A bow large enough to shoot many bolts at a time or possibly a heavy rock."

"But how does it operate?" asked Giuseppe. "That picture doesn't show enough."

"I've read about these machines in another place," said Patrizio. "The drawing doesn't show it well, but I'm quite sure the spring force comes from multiple twisted strands of rope."

"Oh, yes, there on the sides," Giuseppe put a finger there to point it out, "that appears to be the place where the ropes coil."

"What do you think, Giuseppe? Can you make one?"

"I can make anything out of wood, my lord. How big do you think it should be?"

"We will need plenty of power. For that, each arm needs to be at least two meters long. Make them longer, to be sure."

"I'm no carpenter, Patrizio. I still don't really understand how you want to use it once it is made," said Uberto.

"Here's the idea," he answered, speaking to all three of them in a somewhat hushed voice. "They are going to be using their catapults to launch heavy rocks against our fortifications to try to break through the walls. I know their machines are capable of striking from great distances, further than our archers can shoot at them. With this, I hope to be able to push their catapults further and further back, where the damage they can do will not be as great." Turning to Uberto, he said, "You, Uberto, I have chosen to be the one to aim it. You will have help in its operation."

Patrizio's eyes seemed fixed on him, and Uberto's first inclination was to decline. He knew nothing about how such a machine worked, but on second thought, neither did anyone else. Probably it had not been used since Roman times. Then he thought about the men who would be forced to operate the enemy catapults. Men of Renzo's manor, people he had pledged Tiberio that he would protect.

"Sir, you know that it will be our own people whom they will force to operate the machines."

Patrizio sighed, and rising from his seat placed a hand on Uberto's shoulder. "I know that, brother knight. I have thought much about it. There may yet be a way to save some of them. In fact, the ballista may make it easier for us." He turned to Giuseppe and his assistant.

"Giuseppe, I know this is not easy, to make something you have only seen in a picture. You will need help, because I fear there is not much time before they begin their bombardment."

"For this job, I am sure I will have no trouble getting other carpenters. My only concern is that we do it right, so that it is a workable machine. Sire, would you be willing to visit my shop as we get to the important parts of the design?"

"Yes, yes, Giuseppe, I will be there."

Chapter Twenty

The night passed without incident, though hardly anyone slept soundly. Giuseppe, and his carpenters in particular, were busy working through the night on making the ballista. When Carina woke from her fitful sleep, Uberto was already gone; she knew he had the early guard shift. She looked down into the courtyard, and, except for armed knights, few others were to be seen. Everyone had been told to stay inside, or near the walls as much as possible to avoid being struck by arrows when the attack came. However, when it did come, they were to be ready to throw water on the fires set by their flaming arrows.

Why didn't they attack? She wondered. Were the Saracens hoping that on further consideration the town would surrender? That would never happen. She took her sword down from where it hung on the wall. With that, and the dagger Uberto had given her, she vowed that even if the worst came, they would not take her alive.

Then she heard it, a thud. Did she feel a barely perceptible vibration? A second time it came. She looked up and ran out of their apartment. Already, in the courtyard, people were milling about. Again, it came. They already knew. It was what she feared. The attack on the walls of the town. She went to find Uberto.

She moved quickly past other people, going south, toward where she believed she would find him. "Uberto!" she called out when she saw him. He turned away from the wall toward her.

Reaching for her, they embraced, but then he held her away from him, saying, "Carina, you should not be here. They could shoot arrows toward us at anytime."

"But you are here."

"Yes, and I and my brother knights are charged with protecting the city. Besides, we have armor. Go back quickly, Carina, inside, where you will be safe."

"Is it safe anywhere, Uberto? Will they break down our walls?'

"The walls are thick. Let us hope and pray they will hold. Please, go back, Carina. I am afraid for your safety when you are here, unprotected."

"Oh, my husband. You see all these people gathered around the boiling pots in case the enemy attacks. Is it your will that I cower inside, where I can do nothing? I would be with the people of Nice, ready if the attack begins."

"Carina, if you must be outside where there is danger, stay by the parapet, where, there at least, an arrow cannot reach you. And don't do what you did when they attacked before."

Her eyes opened wide when he said that. Clutching his shoulders, she looked wonderingly into his eyes. "Uberto, do you remember? Has your memory come back?" She gazed intently at him, and he shook his head, seemingly trying to recall.

"Yes, Yes some of it is coming back to me. You fell, while fighting a warrior trying to scale the wall. You fell and were captured. I do. . . I do remember—but only a little."

"Oh, Uberto! Do you remember what happened then?" She waited with rising hope as he lowered his head and closed his eyes.

"I don't. I can't. I'm sorry. Somehow you were rescued, but I don't remember how."

"Don't be concerned about that, Uberto. Your memory is returning, a little at a time. That is wonderful."

"Hopefully. I want to remember everything about you."

"In time, Uberto, you will. I believe it with all my heart." Taking his hands in hers, she pulled him close and kissed him. It did not matter to her that others were around to see.

"I will remember, especially because of you. Take courage, Carina. The walls are strong."

She left, looking back at him.

Uberto thought about what he had told her as the rocks continued to crash into the walls. Yes, the walls are strong. But how long would they withstand the constant pounding? He thought about Patrizio's Roman fighting machine. Would it really work, and would it be ready in time? Every minute, it seemed, another boulder smacked into the wall. How long would it take them to break through? A messenger reached him, telling him to come immediately to the war chamber.

He went quickly, pausing only to remove his leather helmet before opening the door. Light gleamed into the room from the open shutters at the rear, and as his eyes adjusted to the low light level, he saw the others already seated around Count Leonardo's dark, rectangular table. He noted the standards and battle regalia to the back of the room before taking a seat and acknowledging the others. Seated there, besides Leonardo, were Patrizio, Donato, Corrado, Heribert, Renzo and a thick set man whom he didn't know.

"Now that Uberto is here," said Leonardo, "we can begin." Speaking to Uberto, he added, "I think you know everyone here except Pippo, Nice's master stone mason."

Uberto sat down next to Patrizio on one side and Pippo on his left. In the momentary silence, he heard the continuing battering going on outside.

"Pippo, tell them what you told me.

Pippo looked at those sitting around the table. "Honored Counts, Leonardo and Patrizio, and honored knights. The walls of Nice are strong, in most places four to five meters thick. Heavy cut stone, a meter thick forms the outer wall and similarly the inside wall. Between them is smaller rocks of all different sizes, a loose fill. On top is the paving we walk on, and at the outer edge, above all is the parapet that protects children from falling and us from the arrows of the enemy."

Pippo paused, and in the momentary silence came the loud wail of a child crying. Leonardo stood up on hearing his daughter's cry, then immediately sat down again, shaking his head. His baby already seemed to want to add something to their discussions.

"We need to do something to stop them!" Pippo's sudden burst of emotion was felt by everyone. He continued. "The enemy is sending all their boulders against one section of the wall trying to break it down. Their accuracy seems to be improving. I have looked at it myself. So far, the wall is holding, but I cannot say for how long." Pippo lowered his head and sat down after delivering his report. Then he looked at each of the others, seeming to hope that someone there had an answer.

Leonardo spoke next. "Pippo, are you saying there is imminent danger that they will soon be able to break through the outer wall?"

"Yes, my lord."

"And the inner wall, apart from the loose fill, will it withstand much of a pounding?"

"I can't say, exactly. If they break through the outside, then some of the fill will likely fall out. The pavement above is supported by that, and it could tumble through as well."

There was silence as every knight thought about the life and death consequences of a collapsed wall.

Patrizio stood up. "Sires, I have been working with Giuseppe, who most of you know is a master carpenter. From the plans I gave him, he is at this time in the process of making a ballista. It is a Roman weapon capable of throwing bolts over long distances. I checked with him this morning. I believe it will soon be ready to be tested against the enemy. If it works, we should be able to drive their catapults back."

"That is good news indeed, my brother." Leonardo rose to his feet. "Until it can be tested, I have another idea. What if we made a barrier between the walls and their artillery?"

"How would you do that, my lord?" asked Corrado, looking up at him.

"With logs."

"Logs?" asked Corrado, seemingly incredulous.

"They are concentrating their attack where they think they will have the easiest time of breaking through. If we hang logs down from the top at the place where they are striking, the rocks will bounce off, doing little damage."

"Good idea," said Donato. Renzo concurred.

"It seems almost too simple," spoke the gruff voiced Heribert.

"They will shoot arrows to set the logs on fire," added Corrado.

"Excellent idea, my brother," said Patrizio. "A good source of ready-made logs are the pells we have been using for practice. We will sprinkle them liberally with water so their flaming arrows have no effect."

"Yes," Leonardo answered, "and any of their archers that come close, ours will skewer."

The meeting continued a while longer. The main concern, other than the wall, was the risk of scaling and the danger of flaming arrows. However, they were prepared for that, as prepared as they could be, with water ready to put out fires and hot liquids to pour on the enemy as well as notched poles to push back their scaling ladders.

When the parley was over, Uberto, his tour of duty at the ramparts finished, started for his apartment. Patrizio laid a hand on his shoulder.

"Uberto, before you go back, come with me to see how Giuseppe is coming with making the ballista."

They walked the short distance to his carpentry shop and saw Giuseppe through the open shutters of his front window. He saw them as well. He called out to them.

"Aha, my lord and knight. You have come at the perfect time. It is finished!—I think."

Entering the door, Uberto saw Giuseppe, his hand open toward the machine, and his assistant, both smiling.

Patrizio looked at the ballista, so big it took up most of the front of the shop, and then at Giuseppe and Uberto. "Giuseppe, you have brought an ancient machine back to life! And in so short a time! You are amazing."

Uberto, too, was impressed at how closely it seemed to follow the lines of the drawing.

"Thank you my Lord. We are just finished and have not even had the chance to try it out. We did make these bolts for it." He turned to a bench on the side to show them.

"Let's see how it works," said Patrizio.

"It's heavy. Maybe, with all four of us lifting," said Giuseppe. "First, I have to unbolt the arms so we can get it through the door."

They got it out, and tested it by shooting into the cemetery. Then, with the aid of passersby, Uberto, Giuseppe, and his assistant began carrying it through the streets to the ramparts facing the enemy. Even with eight people, it wasn't easy going, taking a longer time than expected. By then, Patrizio had long since left.

Now, placing it in position, they were ready to try it on the enemy. As not enough bolts had been made, they decided to use rocks. A cart was quickly loaded with them and pulled alongside the ballista. Wotano loaded a rock into the sling, and Uberto cranked the windlass, drawing the big arms back into firing position. Having only used the machine twice when they fired toward the cemetery, he and Wotano adjusted the incline, aimed, and fired. The rock flew through the air, but where it landed, they had no idea.

"I think you shot it too far," said Giuseppe.

"Did you see it?" asked Uberto.

"At first, and then I lost track of it. I think it was heading too far out."

"OK," said Wotano. "I'll lower the incline."

While he did that, Uberto got another rock from the cart and began cranking the windlass. He hoped he was on line with the catapult, for darkness was already falling and before long they would have to wait for the light of the next day.

"Ready, aim, fire," he said, and pulled the pin holding the pouch with the stone. He moved to the right, so he could try to follow the course of the stone.

"Did you see it?" he asked Wotano.

"I lost track of it, but look, there seems to be a lot of activity around the catapult."

"Good, maybe we're on target. Let's keep it up while we can still see before dark."

Uberto and Wotano worked together to keep the ballista firing, changing the machine's direction and altitude slightly each time.

Patrizio came back to see his machine in action. "My God, its working! You are driving them back. See all the enemy troops surrounding the catapult? They're moving it back. Congratulations!"

"The tribute is yours, my lord," said Uberto.

"And to you and Wotano, and certainly to Giuseppe, who from a drawing made this machine."

"Wotano, let's redirect this and see if we can't push back their other catapult while there is still enough light to see."

The two of them, with Patrizio helping, pushed hard on the heavy machine, lining it up as best they could with that of the enemy. Wotano lifted a heavy rock from the cart, securing it in the pouch. "OK," he said, "draw it back."

Uberto was starting to get a feel for how to aim the weapon. "Wait. That one is further out and with the heavy rock you put in, I think we need to raise the elevation."

"I'll crank it up a bit," answered Wotano. "You tell me when to stop."

"That's it. Right there. Give me a minute to draw back the bow and we'll see if we can give them a scare."

The three watched as the rock flew through the air toward its target. None of them could follow it all the way, as the dusk had deepened. Then Patrizio said, "You did it! Look at all the commotion down there. I think you landed that one at their feet."

Uberto smiled, pleased with himself and Wotano. "Quite a weapon you've had made for us, my lord. I am just beginning to feel I know how to use it."

With darkness descending, he and Wotano, with the help of two others, moved the machine closer to the wall to protect it from enemy arrows. Even with the success of the afternoon, Uberto was not at ease, wondering what the Saracens would do next. After a long day, all he wanted was some food and to join Carina, his newfound wife. He looked forward to getting to know her better, again.

* * *

Carina was just finishing up in the room she was using as her workshop. She had let the girls go, and now was leaving, closing the door behind her. Stepping out she listened, surprised. The sound of rocks hitting the walls of the city were gone. Quickly, she rushed through the hall and down the stairs to find Uberto. She knew of Patrizio's machine and of Uberto operating it. Had he stopped their stone throwers?

She made her way through the crowd of people in the courtyard. Had not all of them been told they should not be in the open, as arrows could fly at anytime? Reaching the stairs between the houses that led to the ramparts, she hurried up, looking for him. She spotted the machine. Had it been moved? But she didn't see Uberto. Where was he? In the growing darkness she continued to look for him. Despite the siege, her hopes were high for the two of them because at last some memory of their life together seemed to be returning to him.

"Carina!" she heard him call to her.

She turned toward the sound of his voice. "Ah, there you are."

He hurried to her and they embraced.

She held him tight and then, still holding him said, "I worry for you. You throwing rocks on them. I am afraid they will throw them at you."

"It is the enemy who is scrambling to get out of the way. Patrizio has resurrected a wonderful machine."

"Come. Let's go to the hall while there is still food there. You had no breakfast and no supper. You must be famished."

"I had some. . ." His words broke off, for suddenly flaming arrows lit up the night.

People were yelling and Uberto pushed her to the ground. Carina couldn't see, with Uberto's body covering her. "Uberto, are they attacking?"

"Crawl with me toward the wall, where there is some safety."

A scream pierced the air and the trumpets sounded, warning everyone that the attack was on.

Reaching the wall, Carina looked into the city and saw the barrage of flying arrows. Uberto stood up cautiously, checking to see if the enemy was attempting to climb the walls. He ducked down quickly as a flaming arrow flew over his head.

"Under the cover of night they have come close to release their arrows. But now our own archers are striking back at them."

"Look!" she said, pointing. "That house is on fire."

"And there's another," he answered. "See. Already people are rushing there with water to put it out."

A heavy boulder flew over their heads and with a crack landed on the pavement. Then came another.

"Let's get out of here. They are firing the catapults, not at the wall, but over the wall."

Carina reached out for his hand and they ran together, hunched over toward a spot along the parapet a hundred meters away where others also hid from the continuing attack. Again, Uberto stood up to check on the enemy, and bent down again next to her.

"Carina, you have to get out of here, back to the fortress where there is some safety."

"No, no Uberto. I need to stay here with the others in case they start trying to scale the walls."

"Carina, you know what happened the last time they attacked Nice. Your bravery may have helped with the defense, but cost your father's life."

Carina stared at him, his face indistinct in the darkness. She shuddered, and remembering her father, bowed her head, the tears now coming freely. She whimpered, "How can you say that to me, Uberto?"

"I'm sorry, Carina," he said, taking her huddled body into his arms. "I don't want to lose you."

One hundred meters away another rock struck, and then there was a woman's scream. Carina jumped up and, leaving Uberto, went to offer assistance. It was brother Paul, and Angela.

"Angela, Angela, talk to me," said Brother Paul as he hunched down over the body of the girl.

"Is she alive?" Carina asked. Her heart went out to the girl who had already suffered so much.

Brother Paul took her arm and put his hand around her wrist. "Yes, yes, she is alive.

"Let's get her on the stretcher." They quickly lifted the light girl onto the hide, bordered on both sides by stout poles. "I will help you carry her back. I didn't see any blood. Do you know how she was hurt?" she asked, as they carefully took her down the steep stairs.

"A rock, a big rock hit her. God bless her. She doesn't deserve this. We were going to bring back the wounded. God bless. God bless. God bless. She is so innocent. Why, oh God? Why?"

Carina could see the man was distraught, and as they passed a still burning fire, that tears were streaming down his face. "God willing, she will recover, Brother Paul." She felt the man's sorrow, for it was hers too. With her own hope rising, she added, "Have faith, Brother Paul. Oriana and Talia will do all that they can."

Silently, through the empty street and courtyard, they carried Angela. Going up the steps of the stronghold, they went down the hall toward the apartment next to Oriana's, where, even before entering, they heard loud crying. Going inside, they saw Talia and Oriana tending the sick. The cries were that of a woman and her daughter at the bedside of a man with an arrow in his side.

Looking up, Talia saw them. "Carina! What are you doing. . .?" Then she saw who they carried. "Oh my God! Angela. Here, lay her here," she said, quickly removing blankets from an empty bed. They set her down, and Talia looked down at the girl, checking to see in the rather dim light what happened to her. "Is it her head?" she asked, laying her hands on her bruised skin.

"Yes, yes," spoke Brother Paul. "We were making our way to find another casualty when a rock came up over the wall. It hit her there, on the head. She has said nothing since."

"She has a pulse, though slow," added Carina, bending down to look at where she was struck.

"Thank God for that," said Talia, one hand caressing Angela's head.

"Will she," Brother Paul hesitated, "Will she wake up?" he asked in a whisper, sorrow etched on his worried face.

There was no answer, and Brother Paul spoke louder. "Talia, will she.. ..?"

Carina saw that Talia did not look at him, but lifting her eyes heavenward said, "We must take this hour by hour."

Carina had seen enough. Already, the sights of the sick rooms and the cries of those for the man with an arrow in his side, were beginning to make her sick. "Are there others who must be brought here, Brother Paul?

"I think so."

Talia turned to face Paul. She stood taller than him, and clutching him by his shoulders, she whispered, "We will take care of her, Brother Paul. Pray for her as you go. I hope there are not many more." Turning to Carina, she added, "It is a man's job carrying the sick, Carina. Surely there is someone besides you who can help."

"Perhaps." She left with Brother Paul, but told him to wait for her while she went into her apartment. She came out with her sword in its scabbard, affixed to her side. Now, she felt ready for whatever would come. Brother Paul looked down at her sword, a quizzical look on his face. She grasped the front of the stretcher, saying nothing to him.

Glad, when they left the stronghold, to see no arrows flying, she and Brother Paul returned to the rampart. Patrizio saw them, and she saw him look at her with surprise.

"Carina, you should not be carrying a stretcher. Brother Paul, you will be of more help with Oriana and Talia." He called out to two of the pikemen, telling them to take their place. He said to Carina, "They will only be of help if the enemy manages to scale the walls. Carrying wounded people is not the job of a lady."

Carina gladly gave up the leather carrier to a burly man who took it from her. "Thank you, Patrizio. I was only doing it to help when Angela was struck."

"Angela? The poor girl helping Talia and Oriana?" He seemed suddenly very concerned.

"Yes, she was struck by a rock when helping Brother Paul with the stretcher."

Patrizio seemed taken aback. "We have all these pikemen standing with nothing to do and a mere girl is sent to carry the wounded. Do you know how she is?"

"She was unconscious, that is all I know. God willing, Talia and Oriana can help her."

"Yes, yes. God willing. The attack seems to have ended for now. I will go there."

Carina had no idea why Patrizio seemed so concerned about a peasant girl. Did he know her sad story? Yes, she thought, that's it. Talia has told him. She let the thought go. She wanted to return to Uberto. Where was he? Along the walls, huddled groups of people. They were there if needed to repulse any attempt to scale the walls. Cauldrons of boiling water, liquid animal fat and other noxious substances stood ready to be poured on any Saracen who made the attempt to climb over the parapet. She recognized people from her own manor. There, close to the wall, she saw Gina, her two children and Anna, Talia's young sister.

"Gina, what are you doing here? You should stay safe inside with the children."

Gina appeared distressed, hardly knowing what to say. Finally, she blurted out, "Lady Carina, my husband is out there!"

Carina looked at her with concern. "Do you know that, Gina?"

"Oh, yes, Lady Carina. I have heard what is being said. That they are using the young men from the manor for their rock throwing machines. My husband is young, and very strong. How can I hide inside when he is out there?"

There was nothing that Carina could say to her. She could only hope and pray that somehow Gina and her husband would be reunited. Moving on, she continued looking for Uberto.

At last, she found him, moving along the wall, looking down at the enemy. "Uberto! Uberto!" she called. He turned, smiling, as she rushed into his arms. She held him tight, his arms wrapped tightly around her. "Uberto, I worry so much about you," she said, backing away enough to look into his eyes. "You look so tired."

"Thank God, you are well," he spoke softly to her. "I heard that Angela was struck. The poor girl. Do you know anything more of her?"

"She is in Talia's care. I do not know anymore than that. Uberto, you need to come back to our apartment. I know you have not had any sleep since yesterday."

"Maybe I can. Carina, I think Patrizio's machine has done its job. The enemy rock launchers have been pushed back. I think when the morning comes, we will not find them within the ballista's shooting distance."

"Because of your shooting skill then, my husband." They began walking together hand in hand and came to the steps going from the rampart down to the town. "You have driven them back."

"It came to me after a while how to angle it for distance. But I worry, Carina. We have won one day. What will they try next? When will they strike again?"

As they walked along the town street, they saw that the fires were now under control; only a few flames were still visible. Few people could be seen in the shadowy darkness that was illuminated only by a half moon and a few bright stars. Carina knew that many of the knights and pikemen remained on guard at the walls, and that along with them, common citizens brought their mats and also bedded down—ready if the enemy should attack again. Others were back at home, in fear trying to sleep to renew their energy for what might come.

At last, they arrived back at the apartment Leonardo's steward had assigned them. Carina did not light a candle, but even in the darkness, she could sense that Uberto was tired. She knew he had not slept at all the night before. She helped him remove his hard leather armor, and then actually pushed him into the bed.

He looked up at her, and in the darkness she thought she could tell he had a smile on his face. "Dear wife, you would put me to bed? I am not so tired that I would take your place." He got up and stood on the side. "Get in bed," he said.

To Carina, it seemed like an order. She sat on the edge of the bed and quizzically looked up at him without saying a word.

"See," he said. "My sword goes next to the bed, as always, so if necessary I know exactly where it is in the darkness and can use it to protect you."

Carina lifted her feet from the floor and put them on the bed, still eyeing Uberto's indistinct figure with a bit of wonderment. Then she moved to the side where she usually slept since the day he came back to her. When he seemed to delay, she said, "Come, Uberto, you need your sleep." She patted the bed next to where she lay. At last, he came to lie down beside her. Her arms reached out to hold him. He held her as well, and then he pulled her close, as he slowly began kissing her tenderly, passionately. As he continued with his kisses and more, Carina's breathing came faster, and her heart lifted in her breast. The thought came to her, *He is beginning to remember.*

Chapter Twenty-one

Patrizio was up at first light, taking his usual walk along the perimeter. This day was different, as guards were stationed every hundred meters in defense of the city. There was much on his mind, and he purposely lowered his gaze so as not to be greeted. He preferred quiet in the morning.

He was pleased with the success of his hastily made ballista, and also glad he had chosen Uberto to operate it. It didn't take the man long to learn how to make adjustments so that the stones it threw landed near or on target. That was a great success. So far, the bombardment of the walls had ceased, but who knew when they would start up again. Patrizio realized Nice was up against a shrewd enemy, one who was used to victory. What the enemy would do next was on his mind and everybody else's.

As he walked, he thought about Angela. He had seen how she avoided even looking at a man. Talia had told him about her, how the poor waif was raped and beaten before finally being led into Nice by a knight and his daughter. Patrizio was not usually one to dwell on the injustices of the world, but this particular girl affected him. When he learned she had been struck he even went so far as to talk to Talia to see how she was doing. Unfortunately, Talia told him there was little they could do for her, aside from putting cool compresses on her head to help reduce the swelling. The girl was still unconscious. As he walked, Patrizio did something he didn't often do. He petitioned God to help her.

He continued to walk, and aside from occasional low tones of guards talking to each other, all was quiet. Except that now the birds were waking, chirping to welcome the dawning of a new day. Then he heard something from below. In the quiet, did he hear voices? Carefully approaching the wall, he cautiously sighted over it, but did not see anyone. Again, the sound came. This time, Patrizio was sure he heard a human voice. Taking a personal risk, in the event that enemy archers were below, he again peeked over the wall at the ground below.

Then, he saw them. At least a half dozen men. Men wearing the clothing of peasants—not the conical helmets and chain mail of the enemy. Could they be the captured men from Renzo's manor?

Seeing his head above the wall, they called quietly to him. Instantly, Patrizio realized their situation. He signaled to them to wait and quickly got the attention of a knight on guard duty. Together, they rushed to where he knew there were ropes, and returning to the wall they hurled them to the men waiting below. Patrizio understood the extreme need for silence. If any Saracen heard or noticed what was going on, the men below would be butchered on the spot. Even if they saw them ascending the ropes they could easily dispatch them with arrows.

The knights he enjoined to help with the ropes pulled, and quickly the first man was brought up, a huge smile of joy on his face. Quickly and quietly the ropes were thrown down, two at a time, to bring them up faster. Then a loud cry shattered the morning stillness. They had been discovered! In moments, Saracens rushed toward the men still on the ground. "Faster! Faster!" Patrizio urged the knights. He looked over the wall as the last man grabbed onto the rope. The man scrambled away from an enemy sword, pulling himself up hand by hand even before the rope was lifted. "Hurry!" yelled Patrizio as he looked down and saw the enemy closing in on him. Fortunately, he didn't see any archers among them.

"Pull!" he yelled, as the rope stopped. "What's the matter?" He saw the four knights straining, but the rope didn't budge. Looking over the parapet he saw why. Two of the enemy also had gripped the rope and a third and forth were rushing toward it. Nevertheless, the last of those to be rescued was managing to ascend, steadily pulling himself up

"They're behind you holding on," Patrizio said to him. "Do you have the strength to climb up yourself?"

"I don't know," came the breathless answer.

"Try. Try, and when you get close, we can help you over." Patrizio was afraid that if anyone else pulled on it the rope would break. He grabbed hold of it himself, adding his weight and strength to the four knights already keeping it from being brought down.

"Help me," came the desperate cry of the man, his voice now sounding to be just on the other side of the parapet.

"Hold tight, men. I'm going to let go of the rope and try to grab him." Patrizio did that, and leaning over the edge grabbed one arm and heaved. In a moment, the man was on the ledge and in the next he had dropped down to the ground. He got up immediately, thanking Patrizio and the others profusely, and clasping Patrizio in a strong embrace. Patrizio turned toward the wall, concerned that the enemy might climb the rope. They were gone, but an arrow whizzed over his head. He was thankful the men had been saved before the archer appeared.

* * *

Carina woke up early because of her husband. He had left their bed and in the darkness was putting on his clothes and armor to go to battle. In fact, he was just opening the door to leave. "Uberto," she said, rising quickly from their bed. "Wait. Kiss me before you go."

Uberto returned, and taking her in his arms planted a warm kiss on her lips. "You know where I will be, at the ballista. Visit me, but stay close to the wall where they cannot strike you."

"I will. Be careful, Uberto. Watch for their rocks and arrows."She held him tight again before letting him go.

Carina didn't know what she would do now. Later, she would go to her loom. She would continue to work there, knowing that much more cloth for bandages might be needed. But now, it was too early for her helpers to come.

She wasn't yet hungry. An idea came to her. She and her assistants had already made up many cloths and bandages for treating the injured. She would go to her workshop, put them in a big bag and take them to Oriana and Talia. By now, they would likely need more of them. Besides, she wanted to see if Angela was any better. *Poor Angela*, she thought to herself.

It didn't take long to get her stuff together at her workshop, and athough the bag was large, it wasn't at all heavy. Walking down the long hall to Oriana's she heard moaning coming from the spare room where the injured were being cared for. She knocked first on the door. When no one came, she quietly opened the door.

Immediately, the smells of medications assaulted her nose, and in the half-light of morning coming through an open window, she saw six pallets with people on them. Turning around, she saw another immediately to the right of the door.

Then a door opened from the adjoining room. In came Talia and Brother Paul, both of them carrying things. Talia saw her immediately, and setting her pitcher and other objects down on a small table, she came to her.

"I brought these bandages and cloths for you," said Carina, setting her large bag down on the narrow space between two of the beds.

"Thank you so much," Talia answered, giving her a quick hug. "We will be needing them for sure."

Carina couldn't get her mind off the man on the other side of the room moaning. She nodded toward him and asked, "Is that man going to make it?"

Talia looked toward where she nodded. "Guido? Yes, he's probably the least injured person we have."

Carina shook her head in puzzlement. "How is Angela? I hope she is getting better."

"So sad, that she of all people was struck. But see, there is Brother Paul with her now. He talks to her. She hasn't opened her eyes yet, but she does hear him. I have even seen her grasp his hand in hers when he is with her. We hope, Carina, and pray."

"Oh, I do so also," said Carina. Not having much stomach for sickness, she left. It was time to open her workshop, for soon her helpers would be there. By this time, the morning sky was brightening, and she heard voices in the hall near her work room. Arriving at the door in the still shadowy corridor, Gina was already there, wrapped in the arms of a man. Kara was at her side, jumping up and down.

"Dada, Dada, Dada!" She cried out. Then, Carina realized who it was. She watched as the man bent down and grabbed the girl, bringing her up into a three person embrace.

"Oh, my husband!" cried Gina. "You are safe, thank God!" On seeing Carina, she cried out, "Carina, Carina! Gottfried is back. My man is safe!"

"Oh, how wonderful! I was so worried for him, and for you as well. Thank God." Carina watched as Gottfried set down his daughter and lovingly picked up his son, a toddler, holding him close against his bearded neck and face. The child squirmed in his arms, maybe not quite used to his father yet. Carina told Gina, "Take the day off, Gina. You need time to be with your reunited family."

"Thank you so much." In her thankfulness, she gave Carina a big hug.

Of course, Carina knew such behavior was rather forward for peasantry, but she was used to Gina's effusiveness and smiled at her joy.

Shooing them away with her hands she added, "Go. Go now and enjoy some good time together. Before the Saracens attack again."

Together, the family left to go down the hallway to their apartment, the baby in Gina's arms. Gottfried turned back to Carina to utter, "Thank you."

Chapter Twenty-two

Uberto had been operating the ballista for the whole day. It wasn't a hard job. His friend, Wotano, had done more of the work of lifting and placing the heavy rocks on the machine that they were firing at the enemy. Carina had brought them food and drink from the great hall, but they both had missed the funeral ceremony and the burial of the three men and a woman who had been killed by Saracen arrows. Carina had told him about that. So tragic for the women, children, and husband left behind. Even where he was, far from the burial grounds, Uberto had heard faintly their cries of sorrow. He reflected. Life is short, and often over all too soon.

That was the bad news, sad, though expected when the enemy is outside your walls. One piece of good news she brought--of Angela. The girl had awakened from her coma and was talking. Furthermore, she was ravenously hungry and was eating. Uberto, and all those who knew of her story were elated that apparently she was going to be all right.

He thought of himself. Of the blow to his head that shattered his memory. That for so long left him not knowing his friends and even his own wife. Somehow, it seemed to him, the haze was beginning to lift. He was beginning to remember some things of his life, and of her. Things were starting to come back to him. Everything was far from clear, but Uberto felt that if he were patient he might someday have full command of what happened in his life. One thing bothered him, especially because he didn't know what it was. It had to do with Carina, about a sorrow that weighed on her. He didn't know what it was, but he vowed if there was anything in his power to do to end her regret, he would do it for her.

"Ready," said Wotano, who had placed another heavy rock in the ballista. Uberto cautiously looked over the rampart, cranked the windlass to draw back the huge bowstring, and let the stone fly. Not that it hit anything. The catapults remained back, good, but out of range for the ballista. From there, their aim was far less accurate than before, and the force with which their missiles could strike was greatly weakened. In fact, Uberto noted, they had not fired a stone for over two hours. "Crank it up higher," he said to Wotano. "Maybe with more altitude we can reach them."

Waiting for him, Uberto sighted, and released the bowstring, sending the missile high into the air toward their machine. In the distance, he saw men scrambling. Maybe they had at least gotten close. Darkness was falling, and soon they would shut down for the night. He looked forward to meeting Carina in the great hall for supper. Then, he heard noise coming from a distance, and cupped his ear to hear better. It sounded like pounding. "Wotano, do you hear that?

"I do. Wonder what they could be doing?"

"I hope they are not building scaling ladders."

* * *

Carina was finishing her work for the day also. She told her assistants, "You have done well today, girls. Thanks to you and my loom, we have made many more bandages for Oriana and Talia. I hope to God they will not need so many."

Like everyone, she feared the worst. Patrizio's ingenious ballista had seemed to work in making less effective their catapults. But she knew the Saracens would not give up so easily. She feared the worst was yet to come. Yet, despite that, she looked forward to supping with Uberto in the hall. He was beginning to seem different to her of late, more like himself. She smiled, thinking his memory was coming back. Such beautiful memories they had shared together.

She delayed, knowing that he would not come until dusk. Then she went back to her apartment, their apartment, and went through her clothes. Clothes mostly that Giancarlo had given her when they were married. She picked out something nicer than what she wore for work. Something that showed more of her skin than usual. She prayed that Uberto would like her wearing it. She knew he tended to be rather conservative about what he wanted to see her in, in public.

In the gathering darkness, Uberto and Wotano could no longer see well enough to orient the machine toward the enemy. With considerable effort, they worked together to push it tight against the rampart, safe from enemy missiles or flaming arrows. Then, together, the two of them went to supper.

On entering, Wotano saw his wife, who had also waited for him, and he went to her. Uberto looked around, and not seeing Carina, went immediately to the long table with the food, picked up a trencher, and helped himself. Turning from the .table, he looked for her, and still not seeing her, he chose a spot where knights and their spouses ate, and sat down alone. It was late, most people had already eaten. Then he saw her, entering the hall from the other side. She acknowledged him with a wave, got a trencher from the table, added some food and went to sit across from him.

She noticed he looked rather long at her garment. "I don't remember seeing you wearing that before," he said.

"Do you like it?"

"It's very pretty on you," he answered, seeming to pay more attention to her bodice than she was used to, at least in public. "Is it something from all the garments that Giancarlo gave you?"

"Yes, it is," she answered, now feeling a bit self conscious.

"I like it. It's just that it shows a bit too much to other people."

"Darling, I'm only for you," she breathed, reaching across the table and tenderly taking hold of his arm.

He smiled. "I'm glad of that."

Changing the subject, He said, "I'm afraid, Carina, that another attack may be imminent."

"Soon, yes, but do you think right away?"

"I don't know if you heard the pounding this evening. Sounded like they were building ladders."

"To scale the walls? No, not again." She lowered her eyes, shaking her head in denial.

"Carina, look at me. I worry about you. I'm beginning to remember more of the past, and now I know how you were taken when defending the walls. Promise me you won't even attempt to push them back with your hands."

"I won't, Uberto," she said, lowering her head once again at the thought of the humiliation she endured, and of what happened to her father. She reached for his hands. "I worry about you, my husband. I know how you are always in the thick of the fray, and though you are a great swordfighter, you cannot see what comes from behind you."

"I will be careful. Most of all, I want to be able to protect you. Changing his demeanor, he added, "But hopefully, Carina, this time they will not succeed in climbing over the wall. We have many more pikemen who will be ready to strike at any that try to climb up their ladders, not to mention all the caustic hot liquids we will throw on them."

"Yes," she answered, but with not nearly the assurance of Uberto. A loud horn sounded. She looked apprehensively into his eyes. It sounded again and again.

"They are attacking! I'm going!" he said, rising quickly from the table.

"I too," she answered, standing up. "First I will get my sword."

"Be careful, Carina. I don't want to lose you now." He quickly rounded the table, and pulling her to him in a tight embrace, kissed her, and then was gone, rushing toward the rampart.

She looked at his rapidly retreating figure, temporarily mesmerized by her thoughts of what had happened the last time the Saracens had attacked. Then, with resolve etched on her face, she went quickly to get her sword.

* * *

Uberto rushed to the the rampart, dodging a flurry of flaming arrows that flew over the walls in such numbers as to wonder how they could all be launched so quickly. He heard the screams of those who had been pierced, and in a few places saw where fires licked at wooden structures. Already, the shouts of those using water to put out the blazes mingled with the cries of the wounded.

But at the top, knights stood ready, as well as the peasants armed with long sharp pikes. Others of the peasantry gathered in tight circles close to the protecting wall but not far from the steaming kettles—the hot, acrid stuff ready to be poured on the enemy.

Uberto felt a kinship with them. They did not have his hard leather armor, which could stop an arrow if it were not a direct hit. His greatest fear, however, was what might follow after the flaming barrage—an attempt to storm the walls and to breach the gate. Prudently, he stayed close to the rampart, not far from where the ballista was parked. He saw Wotano dash from around the front of it, and crouch next to him.

"Good to have you at my side," said Wotano.

"No one I'd rather fight next to than you, brother," he answered, poking him soundly in the ribs.

"Are you thinking what I am?" Wotano asked.

"That the worst is yet to come? Yes. Look, the barrage of arrows seems to be ending."

The horns suddenly began to sound again. This time not the long sound, like an alarm, but short, quick repetitious blasts. Everyone had been trained to know exactly what that meant. The enemy was climbing the walls.

* * *

Carina returned in time to hear the short blasts. Climbing up the steps, she was glad to see peasants with pikes standing all along the wall, ready to pierce anyone

234

who tried to made it over. Those with the stout notched branches were also ready, if the top of a ladder should appear. She rushed toward several peasant women engaged in lifting a hot bucket of something toxic to pour over the attackers. She helped them, and as it contents were spilled out, she took pleasure in hearing the screams of those below.

She looked to her right and to her left, and everywhere she saw no Saracens. The hot liquids were driving them back. Yet, they kept coming, and she and a peasant girl rushed to the cauldron to refill the bucket and haul it to the wall.

But, they kept on coming. Carina was concerned. Would they run out of the boiling liquids? She feared for what would happen then. From the kitchen, men kept coming, bringing more of the hot, caustic stuff. But she sensed they were not coming fast enough. She helped where she could, rushing here or there along the wall, wherever shouts announced that a ladder was being hoisted. She noted, the Saracens were smart, no longer letting them rise over the wall where they could be pushed over by peasants with their strong notched branches. Only the acrid concoctions effectively stopped them, but only for a short time as more of them kept climbing up to replace those who fell.

She heard the shouting again, nearby, and looked around. They were running out of liquids to throw on the enemy. She looked to the right and left, and saw the same thing. Except in a few places, they had run out of the steaming brew. Fearing the worst, she removed her sword from its scabbard and looked around her. The knights too were at ready, they knew what was happening, as did the peasants with their long pikes. The enemy might successfully get over the wall, but they would face stalwart defenders.

As she looked on, more and more of the enemy were beginning to pour over the wall.

On one side stood Uberto and Wotano, swords drawn. They had worked well as a team, protecting each other's back when they faced thousands of Saracens attacking Charles Martel. Thus far, they had not had to use their weapons, the pikemen had speared the first of those coming over the top. Other knights were spread out at ready, and Uberto knew that among them were his old friend Guy and his newer friend, Coco. The sounds of battle, the clash of pikes and screams of the pierced Saracens grew loud as the battle became more pitched. Some of them were now getting past the pikemen who jabbed at their mail protected chests.

Uberto and Wotano entered the fray. Sweet was the scream of the enemy Uberto struck, who fell at his feet, but now the battle became more frenzied as more and more of them kept coming. Trying not to slip on the bodies of the foe, Uberto and Wotano kept fighting, either side by side, or back to back. Charged by the energy of battle, they struck down the enemy again and again. In a short moment of respite, Uberto looked to his left. Shockingly, he saw Carina in the thick of the battle, thrusting her blade into the chest of a combatant. But, behind her, there was one she could not have seen.

"Uberto!" screamed Wotano, and Uberto turned just in time to parry a blow that would have severed his head. Wresting with the Saracen, they locked swords, until Uberto twisted, releasing his weapon in time to thrust it deep into the breast of his attacker. He glanced again at Carina, fearing the worst, and with a joyful heart saw Coco at her side. Coco must have seen the danger she was in and rushed toward her in time to strike down her assailant.

The fighting continued, the cries and the grunts of those fighting mingled with the screams of those sliced or pierced sounding in the ears of the combatants, and Uberto and Wotano often fought standing on the bodies of the fallen enemy. Fortunately, it seemed to Uberto that the enemy was having the worst of it, and, in one brief moment of inactivity, it seemed to him that fewer Saracens were coming up the ladders. As the battle continued, he was sure of it, and now, the knights were carrying the battle, driving the enemy back, cutting them down or pushing them over the wall.

Before long, all along the wall, there were fewer and fewer Saracens, until at last, those few who remained faced a concentration of knights who quickly dispatched them. Then, the cheering began, the raised voices of jubilant knights lifting their voices, cheering their victory and giving thanks to God for beating back the enemy.

Carina had tears in her eyes, why she didn't know unless it was because she had herself killed several Saracens. She was not used to striking down people.

Seeing Uberto come to her, she lifted her arms as he swept her in a strong embrace, raising her up so his eyes were even with hers. He was sweating and she was sweating after the arduous battle, but she cared little for that as his lips sought hers and everything seemed to pause as their lips joined in a deep kiss.

"Thank God you are safe," he said, and she echoed those same words to him.

Chapter Twenty-three

The battle was over, for that night anyway. Much still needed to be done. The knights and some of the pikemen needed to deal with the great number of fallen enemy lying on the ground. Dividing the space into sections, they counted the number in each part and then threw them over the wall. Better there, than within the walls. The enemy could take them away in the night and bury them if they so wished.

They also needed to remove the bodies of the dead knights and citizens and take the wounded to Oriana and Talia. Fortunately, the losses of Nice were small in comparison with those of the enemy. Carina didn't have to help in moving those to be cared for, but she knew Oriana, and Talia would be swamped with so many wounded. Though she knew herself to be squeamish around blood, she went slowly toward where they were being cared for to see if she could help.

Already, in the hallway, she heard the men moaning on their sleeping pads, and caught a flash of Talia rushing back into the main room. She went in, and saw two women she didn't know helping with care for the wounded. *Good*, she thought. Then, Talia came from the side entrance to Oriana's apartment, carrying several things in her hands.

Talia looked at her saying, "Carina, it is good to see you. I have to take these to the men needing them or I would greet you more warmly. Come with me, if you have a bit of time."

Carina followed her until she knelt down by a man whose color didn't look good at all.

"As you can see, we are so busy now, we scarcely have time to talk."

Carina knelt down next to her, and seeing that she was about to change a particularly bloody dressing, she looked away. "Yes, I can see that. That is why I came. I am not very good with blood, but maybe I could help in another way."

"You are the one supplying us with bandages. That is how you help us."

"My girls can do a lot of that on their own, until when I need to use the loom."

Talia quickly finished changing the dressing and Carina was glad the man did not wake up. She stood up and Carina did also. Facing each other, she could see how tired Talia appeared. Then, Talia looked directly at her and said, "Carina, if you would like to, you could help with the food. Especially at the main meal, we could use your help to bring it from the hall and give it to the men who are well enough to eat a regular meal. It would do a lot to save us from having to take time away from their care."

"I would be glad to do that, and I can have one of my assistants come with me."

"Thank you," said Talia, reaching with her free arm to hug Carina.

Carina went back to her apartment. Uberto wasn't there. Was he still dealing with the bodies of the enemy? She was dead tired. The battle had lasted for hours and it was already sometime past midnight. Removing her outer garment, she laid down in their bed, hoping that soon Uberto would come. Before she knew it, she was asleep. However, it was a fitful sleep, as all the bodies, including the ones she had killed came to her in her dreams. Glad she was when she briefly awakened to find Uberto at her side. How could he sleep so soundly even after a battle? She sat up. By the dimness of the starlight that came through the upper window, she watched him as he slept. She smiled. They were safe. They were together .

Uberto slept well and long, after the exertions of the night. When he awakened, Carina was gone, to her workshop, he guessed. The sun was already higher in the sky than usual, and he guessed he had overslept. Yawning, he did his ablutions and dressed again for battle. Due to the time, he skipped breakfast. He assumed he would be back with Wotano manning the ballista. He went to their place along the wall, finding Wotano there waiting for him. Still tired, he waved to him on his approach.

"Ah, you also slept in," he said, smiling. "I just arrived here myself, minutes ago."

"I'm surprised Patrizio didn't send for us."

"Look down there, Uberto. Things have changed a lot for them."

Uberto peered over the wall. The Saracens seemed smaller in number and further away. Their tents were barely visible in the trees, and he didn't see their catapults at all. Then he looked straight down. Surprisingly the bodies of the enemy were still there lying where they had fallen or where they were thrown. "What do you think they're doing?" he asked.

"Don't know."

To Uberto, the enemy didn't look nearly as formidable as before. Why hadn't they removed the bodies of their dead? It had been a cloudy night, a perfect chance for them to do so with little fear of being skewered by arrows.

A messenger called Uberto's name. "Meeting in the war room. Go immediately."

Wotano and Uberto exchanged glances. "Maybe now we will know something," said Uberto on leaving his friend.

Uberto entered the room, and found already seated the old veterans, Corrado and Heribert, whose fighting skills he knew were little diminished by age, and Renzo, Leonardo and Patrizio. Coming through the door soon after him was Donato, who with him and four others had saved Carina when she was captured by the Saracens. Now, two of those men, her father and Giancarlo were dead.

Already, an important discussion was going on. "They are weakened now with their unsuccessful attempt to scale the walls," spoke Leonardo. "I'm for attacking, using knights and pikemen together to drive them to the sea."

"It worked the last time they besieged us," said Heribert, "though if some of them are part of the other force, they may be more prepared for such an offensive."

"They are afraid of us," spoke up Corrado, in his loud, gravelly voice. "They won't even chance removing their dead from near the walls. I agree, strike them now!"

Patrizio, looking straight at his brother, Leonardo said, "Yes, slaughtering them before they were fully awake was successful last time, but our father died in the battle. I fear they will be ready for us."

"Not only that," spoke Donato. "We don't know how many they are. If they are prepared for us, they could draw us away from the walls, while a second force attacks before we can get back."

"Caution, caution," said Heribert. "We dare not chase them far, even if our attack is overwhelming."

"Sue for peace," said Patrizio, in a quiet voice.

"What!?" Came the response from three men, including Uberto.

"Sue for peace," said Patrizio again, his eyes turning to each of the knights there.

"My brother," said Leonardo, "we have already beaten back their strongest offensive. It is no time to give in."

"That is the beauty of it," he answered. "Coming now, it is the last thing they would expect."

Every man there turned to look directly at Patrizio. "I know you have something in mind. Tell us, brother, what you are thinking," said Leonardo.

Patrizio spoke slowly and clearly. "They have taken great losses, such that some of their resolve may be broken. Yet, the enemy is proud, and not used to defeat. The fact that many of their dead lie near the walls unburied may be an advantage to us. We can meet with them, and offer a truce so they can in safety remove their dead."

"But what would that accomplish, my brother?" asked Leonardo.

"Nothing of itself, but there is something else we might offer."

"What?" asked several men at almost the same time.

"Gold," he calmly answered.

"Gold!" echoed Leonardo, shaking his head, as did Corrado and Heribert. Only Uberto, Renzo and Donato seemed interested in hearing more.

"Are you saying give them gold coins if they agree to leave?" asked Uberto.

"Exactly."

Corrado stood up quickly, slamming his fist on the table. "I have fought many battles. I have not and will not give gold to the enemy!"

"Nor I," spoke Heribert, rising from his chair to stand with Corrado.

Patrizio looked up at them from his seat. "Not even to save many lives?"

Corrado and Heribert sat down. Leonardo spoke. "I see what you are saying, but there is no guarantee we can trust them. They might take the money and continue to fight."

"You're right," said Patrizio. "We can hope they suffered enough losses to accept gold as a recompense for their dead. However, if they do continue to fight, we will recover the gold if we win, and if not they take all they want anyway."

"I like the idea," said Uberto.

"And I," added Donato.

"Might save many lives," said Renzo.

"It is a bad precedent," spoke Heribert. "If we give them gold now, even if they do leave, they will come back in a year or less wanting more."

"That is all the time we need to build more fighting machines, to buttress our walls, and to do everything possible to be ready for them." said Patrizio in reply.

"I think it's worth a try," said Leonardo. "It seems we have nothing to lose, but some gold. Of course we will offer them not even half of what we have."

"How do you propose to get the gold?" said Heribert. "I don't think most people would want to give up what they have." He looked toward Corrado, whom he knew was also against the idea.

"We have to ask our people," answered Patrizio. "I'm thinking it should be done in the cathedral. There the bishop can speak to them telling him how important it is that they contribute."

"Do you think he will do that?" asked Donato.

"I'm sure he wants peace, so I believe so," Leonardo answered. "He should also be willing to give up some of the treasures of the church. Also, he can have clerics there to collect and to issue a receipt."

"Maybe you can get gold from some of the wealthy burghers, but most people will have very little, perhaps a gold coin or two—something they would not want to give up," spoke Heribert.

"I know," answered Patrizio. "We can't expect much from poor people. We are the ones who will have to contribute." He turned to look at each man there.

Uberto lowered his eyes. Unlike most knights, he had no gold coins, except the two he had given Carina after their wedding night. Her morning gift. Those he would not ask her to give up.

Then, he noticed that Corrado and Heribert continued to grumble in low voices between themselves. Those two were now in the minority. Personally, he was glad the plan would go forward and hopeful that it would prevent further loss of blood and put an end to the siege.

Leonardo stood up. He asked who would be willing to parley with the Saracens. Corrado raised his hand as did Patrizio and Donato.

"You, Corrado? I thought you were totally against a plan to pay them to leave," said Leonardo.

"True, I am, but when they see the scars on my face and arms they will at least know that we are not afraid to fight."

"You are willing to negotiate with them?" Leonardo asked again, peering at him as if he wasn't sure.

Corrado waved his forearm in dismissal of the idea that he wouldn't be right for the job. "I will talk with them, but I won't be the one to give everything away."

"I will go also," spoke Patrizio. "We can try to reason with them. Having Corrado with us, one who wants to hold back, might be an advantage for us."

"Ok, I'll send messengers to cry out that we are going to meet with them. We don't want our people to think we are surrendering when we raise the white flag."

The meeting adjourned and Uberto went to inform Carina of what was going to happen. She wasn't in her workshop. Gina told him to look for her at Oriana's.

As he approached, he saw men and a woman lying on mattresses in the hall, and he pressed on to her apartment. Knocking, Angela, not Oriana answered the door.

"She is in the next room," she told him without raising her eyes to look at him.

"I'm not looking for Oriana. Have you seen Carina?"

This time the girl looked up at him, the first time he had ever seen her eyes. "She is there too."

Looking past Angela, he saw a door leading there, and striding past her, he entered. At first, he was almost overwhelmed with the smell of sickness, and at all the bodies lying on mattresses on the floor. He saw Talia, kneeling on the floor with a patient, and then Carina, with her back to him in one corner of the room. Carefully walking between the bedding, he came behind her. She turned around suddenly, bowls in both hands.

"Ah, my darling," she said.

Carefully, so as not to have her drop what was in her hand, he embraced her. "There is much to tell you. Will you be here long?"

"Not long. Most have been fed, though some need more to drink. What is it?"

"We are going to raise the white flag."

"No!" she said loudly, dropping the empty bowls on the floor, her hands reaching to hold him. Surely we are not going to surrender!"

"Not that, Carina. Only to parley with them. Don't worry. I must go back. When you are done here meet me at the parapet, the usual place. I was at the meeting and will tell you all."

Carina looked up into his eyes, as if to read his mind. Seeing his calm composure, she said, "Ok, I will soon finish here and join you. Then you can tell me everything."

Uberto went to his accustomed place along the rampart. He could see that already preparations were being made to raise a large white flag and to sound the horns. Carina went toward him. He saw her rushing up the stairs and smiled as she came near. "My darling," he said, taking her in his arms and kissing her there in public. Not good social etiquette, he knew, but she looked so pretty when flustered.

"See. They are about ready. Over there is the flag," he said, pointing to it.

She took a half step back from him, still within his arms and asked, "But why would we want to talk to them if it is not a surrender?"

"We are going to offer them gold if they end the siege."

"Really?" she said, backing away from him. "That is what you leaders have come up with? I can hardly believe it."

"It was Patrizio's idea, and as he talked about it, the plan began to sound better and better. Finally, we all agreed to it except the old guard, Corrado and Heribert. In the end, Corrado said he would be one of those going to talk with them.

"But Uberto, it seems so cowardly. Don't we have faith in God and in our own strength?"

"We do, of course. But you, helping Oriana and Talia, you see how our people are killed and mortally wounded. What is giving them gold compared to more deaths?"

Carina considered what Uberto said, and then smiled, looking into his eyes. "Do you think they would actually leave if we give them gold?"

He smiled back at her. "Hopefully. They have taken many more losses than we have, and maybe returning home with some wealth would be enough for them."

"I hope you are right. My father used to have gold, before the Saracens took it. Me, all I have is the morning gift you gave me. It is precious to me. They are not going to get that."

"I know. Look, they are raising the white flag."

They saw the flag lifted high, and then came the blasts of the trumpets. Soon, from below another flag was raised, also followed by the blare of their instruments. As they watched, the poles of their canopy lifted and before long four Saracens walked beneath it toward the city walls.

Soon, four unarmed men appeared from below. Uberto pointed them out to Carina. "It's Patrizio, Donato, Father Carlo and Corrado."

From the ramparts, the knights and many of the townspeople were watching what was happening far below. For Nice, Patrizio seemed to be doing most of the talking, and they saw that he turned and gestured to the base of the town where many fallen Saracens still lay. On the enemy side, there appeared to be an interpreter, who relayed the message to an ornately dressed man with a white goatee. That man turned to face the three he came with, as if to get their opinion.

"Look," whispered Uberto to Carina. "See, Donato just handed him a wooden box. I think it is the offer to fill it with gold if they leave."

"So much!" she said aloud. "It looks like it would hold my two pairs of boots with room left over. Do we even have so much gold?" She tried to get his attention, but saw him intent on following the action below.

"Look, Carina. They're shaking their heads. They want more. Corrodo, I think it's him, is walking away, back toward the gate."

Carina stood on her tiptoes to see.

"He's going back. Patrizio has turned around. I think he is calling him back."

"I don't care. If that much gold isn't enough then we will fight them until they are all dead!" She said, fuming.

Uberto stood next to her, secretly amused at how much she was upset about the gold. To him, gold didn't matter much, though it was always good to have a piece or two.

For a long time, not much happened below. Finally, it appeared that some accord had been reached, as both parties moved away from the meeting place.

Chapter-Twenty-four

It was Sunday morning. Two days had passed since the meeting with the Saracens. Everyone had been informed that gold would be collected at the cathedral. Mass had just begun, and Carina sat in the pew next to Uberto. So much was going through her mind. First, of course, would they collect enough gold? Not far behind was her concern for Uberto. Though there had been some flashes of recollection for him, would he ever fully remember their life before the blow to his head? Would he ever be her loving troubadour, singing songs that melted her heart? And, beyond that, if the hated Saracens did leave, would Father Einhard come back with a piece of the cross? To give her the very smallest fragment of which Patrizio had said could bring an end to her barrenness.

So much had been going through her mind, that she missed much of the Mass. She came out of her reverie to hear Bishop Gregorio preaching on the need to be generous. From behind the altar, a priest she didn't know brought out the wooden box that the enemy required to be filled along with a Saracen helmet. Carina whispered to Uberto, "Why that?"

"They wanted us to fill an even larger box. A soldier of theirs brought one forward at the meeting. That's when Corrado walked away in disgust. Patrizio told them, to give him the helmet of the soldier and we would try to fill it. That and the box was the most they were going to get. They finally agreed to those terms."

As Bishop Gregorio finished his talk, people from near the front began rising from their benches and going up to the altar. Two lines began to form, and Carina watched in amazement as some knights and shop owners carried pouches of gold that they counted out into the box. She noted Patrizio rose to put in a large gold medallion along with some gold coins. On each side, a cleric sat with quill and parchment noting down how much each person had given. The people with wealth seemed finished, and yet the box was still not full, though the helmet was brimming. Lastly, came the peasants. Most did not rise from their benches, but surprisingly, to Carina, gradually, slowly, a fair number did come to the fore. She looked at them. Even in their Sunday best, they evidenced little of fashion and none of grandeur, and yet they had given what little they had. She fingered the only gold to her name, besides her morning gift, and rose from her seat.

Uberto put his arm in front of her, holding her back. "You are not going to give your morning gift, are you?"

Carina looked down at him where he remained sitting. "No, of course not. Not that. I will give the medallion Giancarlo gave me before he died."

He let her go, and walking with the peasants, she dropped it into the box.

Bishop Gregorio left where he sat at the altar and came to the box. Raising his voice, he spoke to the congregation. "Thank you. Thank you, everyone who has contributed to this very unusual collection. As you may be able to see, the box is not quite full. Do not be concerned over this. I have ordered several of our gold chalices to be melted down. Hopefully, with them, it will be enough. Father Carlo, would you get them?"

Father Carlo rose from his chair and went around to the back of the altar. When he appeared again, he held in his hands four large chunks of pure gold, which those close to the altar could see were melted down goblets. They were the chalices that had held the sacramental blood of Christ. That which was drunk by the priest saying Mass. Father Carlo gave the melted chalices to the bishop, who ceremoniously knelt and added them to the top of the gold filled box. Standing up again, he said to all in attendance. "Now, I think we have enough."

"Carina sincerely hoped so, but she had her doubts. Could the enemy really be counted on to leave once they had their booty? She looked up at Uberto.

"I know what you are thinking," he said. "I pray that this will satisfy them."

* * *

Two days passed. During the time, the enemy had finished removing their dead from beneath the walls and apparently buried them. Though they had not resumed hostilities, the fact that they were still there had everyone on edge. Finally, on the third day they left. Their ships sailed from Nice. Many, including Carina and Uberto thought they would return. For three more days, the town of Nice waited while those who were injured gradually recovered or died. On the fourth day a funeral service was held for all those who had died in the conflict. On the fifth day, Leonardo put out a declaration to all the citizens of Nice that all were invited to a celebration.

In the interim, something happened that was of particular interest to Carina. Father Einhard and four monks returned. She was burning to know if he had brought back a piece of the true cross. The tiniest piece of which she believed would cure her barren womb. She heard that he came late, the night before. Thinking he must be tired after such a long trip, she decided not to disturb him, though someone had told her where he was staying. Instead, she hoped to see him at breakfast or at the midday meal.

At last, she found him. She saw him across the hall. He looked different, thinner, and there seemed something else about him. "Father," she said as she came up behind him as he was leaving the hall. He didn't hear her. "Father Einhard," she said, louder.

Turning, he said, "Yes, child? Oh, Carina. It is so nice to see you."

"Yes, I am so happy you made it back. I was worried for you and the brothers."

"Thank God, we have returned, though as you might imagine, I have stories to tell of our harrowing journey. And, I understand, so much has happened here as well. When you are finished eating, I would be happy if you could tell me a little about that."

"I would be so glad for that, Father. I am not very hungry. I'll just take an apple off the table and we can talk now."

"Lovely, my child."

They left the hall and together went out into the courtyard.

"I have traveled so long with the brothers, it is so nice to be in the company of a beautiful woman for a change."

"Oh, Father, you are embarrassing me. I am quite ordinary looking."

"Not so, child. You are beautiful and your spirit makes your beauty even more so. Be thankful. They are gifts from God."

Carina didn't know what to say to his words. She lowered her head at his compliment. She was not used to such talk from anyone except Uberto, let alone a priest.

"I understand that after a major battle, Nice paid the Saracens a ransom to leave. They must have suffered many losses to accept such an offer."

"Yes, we slew many of them when they tried to climb the walls."

"And Nice, did many of the knights and townspeople die?"

"Yes, Father, sixty-seven so far, and there may be others that may not recover from their wounds."

"I am so sorry for them and their families," he said crossing himself as he spoke.

"Did your brothers all make it back with you, Father?" she asked, looking up at the tall, somewhat slender man."

"Not Pietro, may he rest in peace." Bowing his head, he again crossed himself. "Thank God the rest of us made it back. But how is it with Uberto and Brother Paul?"

Carina was glad he wanted to know about Uberto. Now she would be able to ask him about the delicate subject that most interested her.

"Brother Paul, under the care of Oriana, Talia and Angela, seems to be fully recovered."

"Thank God. I hope he has learned one does not fight the Saracens with good will and crucifixes. And Uberto, is he better? I mean his memory?"

"Thankfully, Father, it seems to be coming back, but very slowly. He has said some things to me at times that no one was likely to have told him." Carina could no longer hold back what was on her mind. She asked directly. "Were you able to find a piece of the true cross for when you start a new monastery?"

Speaking softly, reverently, almost whispering, he leaned toward her, "Yes, Carina, I have."

Carina froze, her heart filling with emotion. She lacked words to speak.

Father Einhard spoke for her. "Yes, Carina, I remember our conversation. I know how you believe the smallest part of it can make a difference for you and Uberto. It well may, and you shall have it. Only the smallest fragment, you understand. But first, it must be consecrated by Bishop Gregorio."

"Oh, Father, I am so indebted to you," she said, beaming at him.

"Your beautiful smile is my reward. I will get a sliver to you right after it is blessed. However, do not tell the bishop or anyone else other than your husband. It will be our secret. And, if it works, let me be the one to baptize your child."

"Oh, Father, you say the most wonderful things." She gave him a sideways hug as she left him, her heart skipping as she fairly danced away. Already, she was thinking of how she would do it. She wondered if she should even tell Uberto? Or would he think it was an improper use of something sacred? Uberto could be righteous about things like that. She wondered. Should she burn it like incense when they were ready to become intimate, or should she place the fragment under the cover of their bed?

She headed back to the hall to have a bit more breakfast before going to her workshop.

"Carina!" It was her brother, Renzo who was also in the courtyard. He spoke out loud as he walked toward her. "Just heard. Leonardo is going to have a great party. To celebrate the departure of the Saracens."

"For everyone?" she asked, walking toward him.

"For all. There will music and food and drink for the townspeople in the courtyard, and for us a great feast and dancing in the hall. It's about time we had some fun in this town."

"Bravo! I agree," she said cheerily as she came to him. She pushed him hard on the shoulder playfully. "I wonder what Antonia will be wearing," she wondered aloud.

"Something silky and a bit too revealing. And you? His demeanor changed and he turned to face her. "Surely you and Uberto will be there."

"Of course. We wouldn't miss it."

"I'm glad. We have all been through a lot, you more than most." Leaving her, he strode in the direction of the stable, "See you then, if not before, sister."

Carina continued to the hall, glad her brother did not bring up how Uberto was doing. She would have told him the same as she told everyone who asked. "He is getting better. He seems to remember a little more."

As she entered the hall, she put those thoughts away. There were far more interesting things to think about—the upcoming feast and dance, and when Father Einhard would give her what she wanted most.

Chapter Twenty-five

Carina looked down at the courtyard from her workshop. She had let her girls go early. They would need time to get ready for the town celebration that would start before dusk. Already, things were being put into place for it. Everyone knew there would be two celebrations, one outside for the townspeople and the other in the great hall. She had learned that besides nobility, knights and their families, the clergy, and also the healers, Oriana, Talia and Angela would join them in the hall. In addition, any of the burghers or peasants who had contributed toward the payoff of the Saracens were also invited. Carina was pleased. With such a crowd, there would be enthusiastic dancing and fun. True, some of the peasants might drink too much, but how often did they have the chance? Such events did not happen often. She was looking forward to the evening.

Returning to her and Uberto's apartment, she removed her garments and washed, with cloths, soap and towels. She wished she had the availability of Giancarlo's special apartment with its bathing cistern. Uberto still had not returned. She put on a fresh under tunic. Then, what to wear? The night would be special, and she wanted to dress for it. Of all the garments Giancarlo had given her, which one should she choose? She knew some of them Uberto would disapprove of, unless she wore them only for him in their small apartment. He liked them, but not for anyone else to see her wearing.

Still, she wanted to wear something special. Something memorable. Especially for him, but for others as well. She looked in her fortunately large wardrobe, the one specially built for her to hold most of her garments. Looking through them by the evening light still coming through the overhead window, one in particular caught her attention. A beautiful empire style gown with a square neckline, having full sleeves, the whole a beautiful cranberry color. Matched with a short white silk jacket she could wear with it or not. It was beautiful!

Uberto entered. "Uberto," she said, coming to hold him. "I am so excited about tonight. And, I have found the perfect gown to wear."

"You look fetching to me just in your under tunic."

"Ah, yes I know, dear husband," she said smiling. "You would find me comely wearing nothing at all. But, tonight is special. This one. Don't you just love this one," she said, holding it up for him.

"It is beautiful. You are beautiful."

"Thank you, my husband. But you. You need to choose something to wear."

"I'll do that as soon as I bathe," he said, already beginning to remove his garments. "Won't be hard to pick something since I don't have much to choose from."

"My fault. You were gone so long. I am going to make that my next project. A fine suit of clothes for you."

"Thank you for your willingness, but you know I don't care much as long as it fits."

Carina smiled at him, eyeing his manly body as he bathed. "Nonetheless, you shall have a fine outfit when I am finished."

"Please, nothing too frilly or royal looking. I'm a knight, not a noble."

"As you wish, my lord and master." She said it softly, smiling at her own words, which he, in his bathing, seemed not to have heard.

Now dressed, they made their way toward the great hall. Even before reaching it they heard soft music being played and caught the aroma of roasting meat. On entering the great hall she saw that it was decorated with red and blue streamers and the soft light of candles in their wall sconces and on the tables. Uberto held her hand as they walked toward one of the tables. They both lifted their hands to friends already seated near them.

Carina was truly excited on this night. Uberto looked so handsome in his dark blue outfit accented by a crimson neckband. She felt beautiful in her empire gown also of crimson with the delicately embroidered white puffed sleeves. At the table to their right and somewhat behind were Uberto's old friends, Guy and Wotano and their wives, Heida and Natalie, each holding a small child. Carina tried not to be jealous of them. Now that Father Einhard had returned with a piece of the true cross, she believed that her womb also would no longer be barren. She was especially happy this night, for soon it would be so.

Many had arrived early. Though the tables were laden with food, the meat, which she knew would be fowl, lamb and perhaps even fish had not yet been brought out. That is, if there had been time to catch them from the sea after the Saracens left.

Antonia came, escorted by her husband Lord Renzo followed by her two children. A maid carried her youngest, affectionately called, "Buttercup." Antonia was strikingly beautiful, adorned in a white gown with dark blue trim and a matching jacket. They came and sat at their table and immediately Carina and she began talking. Gradually, all the other knights, their wives and children came, as well as the clergy and citizens who were invited, filling up the tables placed on both sides of the long, well laden table. Count Leonardo and his beautiful young wife Lucia and their child were among the last to enter. A horn sounded, and Bishop Gregorio rose to extend his blessing over the food and all those in attendance. At last, they could eat.

Carina noticed that soon after the bishop's blessing, Patrizio rushed in, holding Talia's hand, to join Leonardo and Lucia at table. Talia's younger sister, Anna, followed immediately behind. Talia raised her hand to her in greeting and she did the same. Carina was glad that Patrizio had invited her.

As always, on these kinds of occasions, there was plenty of food and plenty of wine. Carina, felt proud sitting next to her handsome husband as they ate. She personally tried not to eat too much, not liking the full feeling it gave her, but she liked the buttery feeling the wine gave her. As they ate, she enjoyed talking at table with Uberto and the others around them. From her vantage point, she had a good view of the hall. She saw Father Einhard and the five brothers, including Brother Paul, at a table to her right. To her left, were Oriana and Angela, seated with burghers and their wives. Carina noted that Angela looked uncomfortable sitting with men at her table, but at least she had no contact with any as Oriana was on one side of her and a burghers wife on the other. Carina mused, the girl was not afraid of sickly men whom she helped to heal, only of those who were healthy. Such thoughts quickly left her as the musicians began to ply their instruments.

On hearing them starting, Leonard stood up at the adjacent table. "I welcome you all my people, to celebrate now that the enemy has left. I, we deeply appreciate all of you for having surrendered your treasure. Do not be concerned. If the Saracens do return, we have already made plans for how we will chase them away. But this is not a speech. It is a thank you to my people. Especially at this time for those who gave from what little they had to give. In honor of you, shopkeepers, burghers and those who till the land, the first dances will be the favorite tunes you most love for dancing." Turning to the eight who would provide the entertainment he said, musicians, when you are ready, let us begin."

A round of applause greeted Count Leonardo's words and almost before the music started again, people began taking the floor. Carina turned to Uberto. "Let's do it, my husband."

"Wait," he said putting a hand on her thigh. "Wait until others besides the farmers join in."

Carina was impatient. She looked around her where sat the knights and their wives. She caught Natalie's eyes, and knew she would be dancing, baby and all, except probably Wotano was reluctant. Why were people of rank so slow to feel the music? Then, at the next table Patrizio rose from his seat, offering Talia his hand, and she immediately stood up. Carina watched as he gracefully led her down the one step to the dance floor. She continued to watch as they joined the others, the two dancing with them as if well practiced in commoner dances. She turned to Uberto, who also was watching their movements, hoping he would now be ready. Too late. Already, the first dance was ending.

The second was like it, and many of the burghers and peasant farmers and their wives had remained on the floor in the interim. Patrizio and Talia did so also, and Carina was turning toward Uberto, when, from the corner of her eye she caught a glimpse of Brother Paul. He had left the monks at their table and was walking toward where Oriana and Angela sat with others. Bowing before Angela, he held out his hand. The girl hesitated while he stood there, and then, breaking into a smile, she took it and joined him. Carina could hardly believe her eyes. The girl who had suffered so much at the hands of men, was now going to dance with one.

A tear slipped from her eye as she turned to face Uberto.

"Carina, what is wrong?" Uberto asked, seeing the tear.

"Nothing, my husband. Everything is right. Come, let's dance."

The next dance was also of the country kind, one that seemed to be known by most. Though starting with pairs, it soon broke into a circular dance, with everyone facing into the middle. Carina and Uberto joined in and they were both glad to see that others of the knights, including Patrizio and Talia, Wotano and Natalie, Guy and his wife, Heida and even Coco and his wife were coming on the floor. Those with babies seemed to have found others to hold them. As the dance ended, she noticed that Father Einhard, the brothers and many of the clergy began standing up as if they were about to leave.

Father Einhard signaled to her, and leaving the others, walked in her direction where she and Uberto waited for the next dance to begin. He held a very small leather pouch in his hand. "This is it, Carina. It is only a very small sliver. Do you have a pocket where you can keep it safe?"

"I don't know Father." She fumbled at her dress, looking for one. She realized Uberto had no idea what he was giving her. "Ah, yes, here is one," she said on finding a small slit pocket. "I can keep it here."

"Good. I pray that it will do all that you wish." Then he walked away to join the monks who were leaving.

Uberto looked at her questioningly. "What did he just give you, Carina?"

Carina was a bit flustered. She had hoped she would be given the fragment of the cross when alone. How was she going too explain it to Uberto? And, how would he react?

She decided quickly that her best course was to be less than fully truthful while still not telling an outright lie. "It is a bit of a relic that Father Einhard obtained while in Rome."

"That was nice of him to get it for you. What saint is it a relic of?"

He asks the hardest questions, thought Carina. *How can I answer?* She decided it was best to be truthful. "It is a relic of the cross," she answered, looking at him full in the eyes.

The music started again, but Uberto, taking her arm, led her back to their table. After they were seated, he asked her, "Do you mean an actual piece of the true cross?"

Carina's head was lowered, but then she looked up at him, "Yes, Uberto."

"Carina, don't you know that is the most valuable thing you could have. I can't believe he gave it to you."

"I think it is only the tiniest sliver, Uberto. A larger piece he has kept for when they build a new monastery church."

"Let me see it."

She took the small pouch from her pocket, and opening it, became alarmed. She didn't see anything. Uberto peered into it where she had it on her lap. "Let me see," he said, taking the pouch from her. "Maybe it is very small."

He opened the pouch wide and brought it closer to his eye. "Ah, there it is. Its brown color blends with the leather. "See it, Carina. It is very small indeed." He handed the case back to her. "You are very fortunate to know a priest who would do something so wonderful for you."

"Yes, I am very thankful." Carina realized that Uberto had no idea of the miraculous power of such a treasure.

"We should take it to our apartment immediately, and then we can come back for more wine and dancing."

"Yes," she agreed.

As they left the hall and made their way back to their residence, Uberto continued to talk about how she, of anyone he had ever known, was now in possession of such a sacred relic. Carina, however, was thinking. She had planned to burn it at just the right time so they could breathe of its healing powers. Now, she knew that would be anathema to Uberto. Instead, she would try to find a way to slip it under the mattress cover when they became as man and wife.

When they returned to the hall, Uberto was smiling, and truthfully, Carina was in good spirits as well, for he did not know her secret of how she intended to use the fragment. He whispered in her ear, "Don't tell anyone about this, Carina. It will be our secret."

Now, the dance was in full swing, and most of the knights and their wives, the burghers and the peasants were on the floor. The buffet tables had been moved back out of the way, and still, they had to look for a place toward the front where there was room to dance. As Uberto took her into his arms, she was happy. She could not help looking into his eyes in a loving, meaningful way.

"What?" he said.

"I'm just so happy. We haven't danced together since before you were injured.

"That's right. I am fortunate to have found my way back to a woman who is so beautiful."

As he held her close, she whispered into his ear, "I love you."

The dance ended, leaving Carina with a dreamy smile on her face.

They sat out the next one to talk with friends and relatives at and near their table and to drink some more wine. Carina glanced out at the dance floor and saw Brother Paul and Angela together. Not appearing to know the steps very well, they seemed to have settled on standing close together, moving their feet only a little. Angela seemed content to look into Brother Paul's eyes, and Carina smiled, knowing they had both been through so much. She was happy for them. She didn't see any reason why Brother Paul couldn't leave the brotherhood if he so desired.

The wonderful evening continued with dancing, some drinking and talk. In time, the women came together on two tables next to each other and the men joined on other tables, both groups engaged in much conversation. So much had happened and was happening. So many changes were afoot. It was not until much later that people began leaving and Carina and Uberto returned to their apartment.

As they began undressing, Uberto was the first to speak. "Have you heard that the consensus among the Leonardo and his aides is that your brother's manor is no longer safe. Most of the knights seem to believe we should rebuild on the outskirts of the walls of Nice.

"Really!" she answered. "That would take a huge amount of work."

"For sure. Definitely would be safer though, for at the first sighting of the Saracens we could hurry into the town."

Carina appeared to be thinking over the news, but she had news of her own. While sitting on the bed removing her sandals, she told him, "Talia thinks Brother Paul and Angela will marry."

Uberto had turned away, unfastening and then removing over his head his handsome outer tunic. Turning back to her, he said, "Really? He would give up being a brother?"

"Yes. Talia thinks it would be the best thing for him. She doesn't think he was ever meant to be one. And Angela. She won't even look at another man aside from him. Maybe it would be for the best."

Uberto faced her, seeming to be taken by her figure in the light of the single candle. "Stranger things have happened. Wouldn't that be a surprise to Father Einhard and the brothers." He came close, standing just before her now.

Carina felt his nearness, and now looking into his eyes, said, "Father Einhard is a quite perceptive man. He may. . ."

Whatever Carina was going to say no longer mattered, as Uberto took her into his arms. Other than Uberto, her only thought was of the small leather pouch on the roughhewn dresser. Somehow, she wanted to get it under the mattress cover.

"We don't need this," said Uberto, beginning to lift off her under tunic.

"I know," she answered, her breath already coming faster. Taking another glance at the pouch laying there, she uttered, "Blow out the candle, Uberto."

He did, and while he finished undressing she took the small leather pocket and pushed it up and under their mattress cover. The thing was practically flat, and she didn't think that Uberto would even notice it beneath them. He took her in his arms. She smiled up at him, before he covered her lips with his own.

Chapter Twenty-six

Two months had passed and so much had happened. New houses erected by the peasants, a new fortress was being built for Renzo, his family and the knights. New land cleared and already partly cultivated with a fall crop, and a new stockade being erected, as Carina looked out on her brother's new domain.

For her personally, an even more important event was going on inside her. She could hardly believe it at first, and as she had been wrong once before, she told no one. Not even Uberto. She did not want him to experience great joy only to be let down. This time, she would be sure before she told him.

She had listened when she heard women talking about their pregnancies. She believed she had the symptoms. Tender breasts, a feeling of being tired, some nausea. Thankfully, she did not have any morning sickness—at least not yet.

She began thinking about Brother Paul. He worked with the monks during the day, but toward evening, he would go up the hill, through the gate and into the stronghold. The guards at the gate knew his routine and would open on seeing his figure. Brother Paul would meet Angela in the hall late, before it closed for the day, and they would eat and talk quietly. Carina had been there one evening when Brother Paul said something that made Angela laugh heartily. She had never seen Angela laugh before. It was good to hear her giggle before breaking out into full laughter.

Once, she happened to be in the hall when he entered her room. That was unusual. Ordinarily, Brother Paul departed after supper and went back down the hill to sleep in the big house with the other monks. She wondered about those two.

* * *

Uberto stepped back to look at the new fortress— the one that would be the home of Renzo, Antonia, Amadeo, and, of course, he, Carina, and the knights and their families. It had been decided that Renzo's manor was too small and outlying to resist a return of the Saracens.

All around him he saw work being done. On one side of the new courtyard, he saw the monks. They had already built a large dwelling for themselves, and now they were laboriously erecting a chapel. A chapel made of stone so that at least it could hopefully withstand a Saracen attack. He had talked to them and knew that in their plans for the future they wanted to open a small school. The children of knights and even some peasant children might actually learn to read and write!

His thoughts went to him and Carina. Somehow, it seemed that soon after the Saracens left he had regained his memory. In fact, as he looked back, it seemed it came back to him right after the feast and dance. Now, he felt he was able to remember everything, including how he had acted so strange when he didn't even know Carina was his wife. Even the words to his music came back to now, and already he had more than once serenaded her with songs in their apartment.

Carina herself seemed a changed woman. The sadness he at times had found in her was gone. Something he couldn't quite fathom seemed lately to be bringing a frequent smile to her lips.

Their anniversary was coming, and though it was not the norm, he wanted to do something to mark the occasion. He didn't yet have money, but he thought of a way he could buy a gift for her. The sword Talia had given him. Now that he had his own sword, one with the emblem of his manor inscribed on it, he didn't need the other any more. Taking the sword, he went to the shop that sold fine things, and bartering, selected something beautiful for her.

He also scouted the land on horseback, looking for a spot not too far away where he could take her. A place where they could be alone and he would sing beautiful songs to her accompanied by his small lyre. A place with a wonderful view. A place he knew she would like.

It was the day, and they set out together. He led her to the spot, one with a wonderful view overlooking a small lake. He had told her, but only the day before, that he wanted to go with her to celebrate their two year anniversary. It was unusual, anniversaries were seldom noted in those times, and the idea caught her by surprise.

By afternoon, riding along together, they reached his chosen spot.

"Oh, Uberto, it is so beautiful here," she said.

"Yes, I looked a long time before finding it for you."

"You are so good to me, Uberto. Surely we were always meant to be."

They dismounted, and Uberto took her in his arms. His face close to hers, he whispered, "Let nothing ever separate us again."

Carina looked up into his eyes, and just before they kissed said, "Never."

Releasing her, he said, "I want to play for you, but first, let's eat. I'm famished.

Carina could have put off eating, in the tenderness of the moment, but she too was hungry and she set about getting out their lunch from the saddlebag. They settled down on a large fallen log overlooking the lake.

There was so much for them to talk about, especially since Uberto had his memory back. Talk about their tumultuous past, their narrow escapes, but also talk about the future. Uberto stopped them, saying, "I want to play for you, Carina."

Carina was glad, for even more than their talk she loved his music, especially when it was directed just to her. He seemed at those times to sing and play with a heart rending tenderness that touched her deeply.

He continued at length, until already the early fall sky began to deepen as evening approached. He stopped, and coming to her, she felt he was going to kiss her. Instead, he retrieved something from his pocket. He came close to where she was sitting, holding it now before her.

She looked down at it, a necklace of beautiful, opalescent, emerald green stones, that even in the darkening sky seemed reflect many colors.

Oh, Uberto! It is so beautiful! This is fit for a queen."

"It is for a queen, the queen of my heart." He leaned forward with a kiss. She moved to be close to him, and arms around each other, the intimacy of their kisses deepened.

Then, suddenly, Carina broke off. "Oh, Uberto, I have nothing to give you in return."

"I need nothing but you," he answered, his eyes still showing the passion he felt for her.

"Yes!" she said as the thought came to her. I do have something I can give you."

Completely surprised, he answered, "What, my lady."

"A child," she answered, now looking intently into his eyes to see his reaction."

"Really? Our child? I didn't think. . ."

"Yes, yes, it's true, Uberto," she interrupted. "I waited so long to tell you, to be sure."

"Oh, my darling, I can hardly believe it. It is so wonderful. Our own child."

"Yes, and if he is a boy, he will grow up just like you, strong, faithful, loving, and maybe he will also play and sing. I would like that."

"And if a girl, let her be just like her mother. "Sweet, beautiful, charming, and spirited. One a man will not take advantage of."

"Uberto, I need you so much. Especially with our child on the way"

"I will always be here for you," he answered, taking her into his arms.

Some history

It may be interesting to know that the story is based on real history. The Saracens are real, and were actually conquering in what is now southern France, where the novel is set. In fact, there are even sketchy records indicating that they attacked the little town set on a plateau that is part of present day Nice.

The record shows that Nice did survive at least one attack, and maybe more than one taking place sometime around 730AD and after

If you should happen to visit Nice, you can climb the stairs or take the lift up to what today is called "Colline du Chateau," or "Castle Hill." This is where the story is set. Today, it is a huge park, which during quiet times you can imagine all that must have gone on there well over a thousand years ago. You can even visit the remains of the medieval cathedral. Or, you can look out over the city of Nice or out toward the port and the beautiful Mediterranean Sea.

I like to think that people like Carina, Uberto, Patrizio, Talia, Angela, Giancarlo and others existed back then. To me, they are like us. Each different, each with strong feelings, strengths and weaknesses. Here, you see them in a novel, but it is my hope that you also recognize them in the people you see today. In different circumstances, they might be that valiant knight or that brave woman.